CW01510382

Billionaire Undeceived

THE BILLIONAIRE'S OBSESSION
Devon

J. S. SCOTT

Billionaire Undeceived

Copyright © 2025 by J. S. Scott

All rights reserved. No part of this document may be reproduced or transmitted in any form or by any means, electronic, mechanical, photocopying, recording, or otherwise, without prior written permission.

Proof editing by Annette Stone
Cover photo by Wander Aguiar Photography
Cover designed by Sarah Kil Creative Studio

ISBN: 979-8-280463-85-1 (Print)
ISBN: 978-1-959932-24-6 (E-Book)

Contents

Chapter 1 1
Chapter 2 9
Chapter 3 17
Chapter 4 24
Chapter 5 32
Chapter 6 38
Chapter 7 45
Chapter 8 52
Chapter 9 60
Chapter 10 68
Chapter 11 75
Chapter 12 82
Chapter 13 88
Chapter 14. 96
Chapter 15 103
Chapter 16 110
Chapter 17 117
Chapter 18 123
Chapter 19 130
Chapter 20 137

Chapter 21 144
Chapter 22 151
Chapter 23 158
Chapter 24 165
Chapter 25 172
Chapter 26 180
Chapter 27 186
Chapter 28 192
Chapter 29 198
Chapter 30 204
Epilogue 212

Chapter 1

Reese

"Devon offered to teach you to ride on Saturday," my boss informed me as we sat in the reception area of the office for Glam Anywhere. "I know you really want to learn to ride, so I told him it was a great idea."

I gaped at the woman who had become not just a boss but a friend to me.

Devon Remington was Hannah's brother-in-law, and she adored him.

I, on the other hand, did not want to spend any time I didn't absolutely have to spend with Devon.

I *did not* adore him.

In fact, he was a huge pain in my ass.

"Why would he do that?" I asked her cautiously.

I was certain that Devon didn't like me, either.

Why would he want to do *me* a favor?

He came to the office fairly often. He probed me constantly about my personal life and my history, something I refused to talk about with him.

My life was none of his damned business, but he tried to make it his business every time he visited Glam Anywhere.

Hannah sighed as she sat in one of the chairs in front of my desk. "Look, I know you don't exactly love Devon like I do, but underneath all of his bullshit, he is a good guy."

I snorted as I closed my laptop. "I highly doubt that Devon is just trying to be a nice guy. He antagonizes me every time he stops by."

It was closing time, and Hannah and I had just finished our business for the day.

I'd been working for the mobile beauty company for months, and the business had grown enormously since it had opened.

We were conquering Montana, but there was still a lot of work to do to make the company go national in the future.

I was the manager at Glam Anywhere, but Hannah was far from an absentee boss. She was engaged in every aspect of her business, and she spent as much time here as I did.

Hannah's husband, Tanner, had tried to get her to work shorter days because her pregnancy was getting more advanced. But Hannah was an independent woman who wanted her new business to succeed. She insisted that she was feeling just fine, but that didn't stop Tanner from checking up on his pregnant wife several times a day. He was a little obsessive, but it was their first child, and I couldn't blame him for worrying about his wife.

"Please just go and let Devon teach you to ride," Hannah insisted. "He really would be a great teacher. He's been riding since his early childhood, and he's a much better rider than I am. I wish I could teach you myself, but I can't ride while I'm pregnant."

I nodded, completely agreeing with her comment. Hannah shouldn't be getting near a horse while she was pregnant. There was too much risk of falls or abdominal trauma. "I can wait," I told her emphatically. "I've lived this long without getting on a horse."

Yeah, I really did want to learn to ride, but it wasn't *that* urgent.

"It would be so good for you," Hannah nagged. "You're relatively new to Montana, and I think you'd love it. You've done so much for me, Reese, I want to return the favor. You've worked so hard with me to get this business up and running, and I owe some of my success to your hard work. You took care of everything while I was on my long honeymoon in Australia. I just want to do something nice for you. What's up between you and Devon anyway? You seem uptight every time he comes in."

Damn! Hannah had been a great friend and boss, and it was so hard for me to refuse to do something she really wanted me to do.

However, Devon was a thorn in my side, and I really didn't want to shove that thorn in any deeper by spending time in his company outside of work.

"Nothing is up," I assured her. "We just don't like each other."

Hannah's expression was solemn as she asked, "You do realize that all of his cynicism and obnoxiousness isn't the real Devon, right?"

I lifted a brow as I looked at her. "It's not? If it's all artificial, he seems to have that act down pat."

"He has a good heart," Hannah replied. "He just doesn't show that side of himself to most people."

Ha! I'd definitely never seen that side of Devon Remington. He questioned me incessantly and never seemed satisfied with any of my answers.

He unnerved me, and that didn't happen very often.

"For some reason, he doesn't seem to trust me," I confided. "He keeps digging at me about why I moved to Montana. I know that he's protective of you, but he can't seem to understand that I'm not here for some nefarious reason. I needed a change in my life. Devon sees that as suspicious because I made a drastic move from the city to a small town in Montana, and I didn't know anyone here when I moved."

Hannah shrugged. "It's a small town. Everyone is suspicious of strangers at first."

I nodded. "I get that, but Devon is taking this to an extreme. Nobody in town looks at me like a stranger anymore. I've lived here for months. I'd like to think most people actually like me."

It was a substantial change for me to move to this small town in Montana after I'd taken the job that Hannah had offered me, but I thought I'd adjusted pretty well.

I liked my job and the people here in Crystal Fork.

Yeah, things moved at a slower pace, but that was a plus for me. It was something I'd needed in my life.

"They do like you. Before long they'll be seeing you as one of their own and trying to fix you up with every single male in town," Hannah answered immediately. "Honestly, I don't know why Devon is being so stubborn. Maybe his offer to teach you to ride is his way of apologizing. Take him up on the offer, Reese. Devon doesn't offer to do anything he doesn't want to do."

Personally, I was sure that he had a motive behind that offer, but I didn't want to offend Hannah by telling her what I really thought.

I also didn't really want to admit just how uncomfortable I was in Devon's presence.

While his older brothers Kaleb and Tanner were friendly and outgoing, Devon was…different.

He held his cards close to his chest, and he was extremely hard to read.

His dark, intriguing eyes seemed like they could see right through me, but I just couldn't judge what emotions were in their depths.

He was sarcastic and annoying.

Unfortunately, the man also intrigued me just a little. If everything Hannah said was true, I had to wonder what had made Devon so different from his older brothers.

Also, unfortunate was the fact that he was stupidly attractive.

He was the epitome of tall, dark, and handsome, wrapped up in a very mysterious package.

"Please," Hannah pleaded. "Just go this once and see how it goes. I think you'll have fun, and something tells me you need a little fun in your life. You don't really get out much, Reese, and that worries me. Maybe I'm a little afraid that you might be regretting your decision to come here to Crystal Fork."

I shook my head. "I don't. I guess I'm just more of a homebody."

Hannah raised a brow. "Really? You live in the same small apartment building I lived in before Tanner and I got back together. There's not much to do in those tiny apartments."

What in the hell could I say to that comment?

Honestly, I'd always liked keeping busy and doing new things, but I had my reasons for wanting to keep to myself these days when I wasn't working.

Unfortunately, as close as I'd gotten to Hannah, that wasn't something I could exactly explain to her right now.

"I like my apartment," I protested. "It's not like I *never* get out. I go to The Mug And Jug, and I frequent your mom's donut shop way too often."

"You've never been to Billings, and I invite you to come every time I go with Lauren and Anna," she reminded me. "In fact, I don't think you've left Crystal Fork since you moved here so you can see more of Montana."

I hadn't.

Maybe that did seem odd since I'd never been to Montana before I moved here for this job.

Normally, I would be curious to visit different places, but my life was far from normal at the moment.

"The weather sucks," I muttered as a pretty weak excuse, wondering how I could get off this particular topic. Maybe if I agreed to let Devon teach me to ride, Hannah would stop badgering me about getting out more.

"It's spring now," she cajoled.

"Okay," I said, desperate to change the topic. "I'll go once on Saturday and see how it goes."

Hannah's face lit up. "You're going to love it. Devon has some incredible horses. I hope you'll figure out that he's harmless and a pretty nice guy once you see through his bravado."

I highly doubted that, but I could get through an hour or two in his company to make Hannah happy.

I felt more than a little guilty because I couldn't share everything about myself with her.

Hannah, Lauren, and Anna had become good friends to me, but I wasn't being entirely honest with any of them.

Anna was an incredibly famous pop star who was married to Kaleb Remington.

Lauren was like a sister to Tanner.

I adored all of my new friends, but there were just things I couldn't share with any of them, and that bothered me.

A lot.

There had never been anything mysterious about me before I'd moved to Montana.

I was honest.

I considered myself a good friend.

So my lack of truthfulness was wearing on me, but I didn't have much of a choice.

"I really don't hate it here," I told her sincerely. "I don't regret my decision to move to Crystal Fork. I was grateful when you offered me this job, and the challenge of getting a new business up and running has been good for me."

At least that comment was entirely true.

Crystal Fork was a quirky small town, which actually appealed to me, and everyone had been so kind and genuine.

Well, except for the man who was a thorn in my side.

I'd never lived in a town as small as Crystal Fork. It had taken some time to get used to, but the longer I lived here, the more it grew on me.

"You've been invaluable as a manager, Reese," Hannah said genuinely. "But as a friend, I worry about you sometimes. I'm not sure why, but you seem a little edgy and cautious at times. I understand that because I lived in Seattle for years. I guess we're just more cautious when we've lived in a metro area. I'm hoping you'll feel more relaxed as time goes by."

"Salt Lake City isn't as big as Seattle," I told her. "But yeah, it's different here."

I'd use any excuse I could find to explain my wariness, and Hannah had given me a good one.

God, I hated my life right now, but I was hoping things wouldn't go on like this forever.

"I'm getting out on Saturday," I added in a lighter tone, trying to stall any further discussion about my lack of a personal life.

She beamed. "I'm overjoyed you're going to learn to ride. You've been talking about it for months."

I'd actually be happy about it as well if I didn't have to have Devon Remington as an instructor.

I'd always loved horses, but I'd never learned to ride. The closest I'd gotten to riding was being led around on a pony as a child.

Try not to let him get to you, Reese.

I let out a long breath and wondered how I was going to accomplish that.

Devon did get to me, and his constant questions about my personal life made me squirm in my seat when he was here in the office.

Something told me that he knew how much it bothered me, which just encouraged him to keep asking more questions.

I was a terrible liar, and it didn't come easy to me.

I was going to have to be a little less transparent and act like nothing he asked bothered me.

My parents had always told me that they could tell when I wasn't being honest with them, and they were probably right.

Maybe I'd stop worrying about *his* questions and start asking a few of my own.

Devon Remington was a mystery to me, and I was a woman who liked to solve puzzles.

If I kept him busy answering my questions, he might not have as much time to start firing off his own.

Hannah looked at her watch and rose from her chair. "I'd better get home. If his girls aren't home before he gets home from work, Tanner starts losing his mind."

I laughed. Hannah was having a girl, and Tanner was already calling them his girls, even though the little girl hadn't been born yet.

"Go," I encouraged, knowing how anxious Tanner was about Hannah's first pregnancy. "I'll lock up."

I watched as Hannah gathered her things and prepared to leave.

She and Tanner had experienced an exceedingly long journey to happiness, but she was glowing now.

It was obvious that Tanner and Hannah belonged together, even though it had taken them a long time to figure that out themselves.

Her pregnancy had gone smoothly so far, and she and Tanner were over the moon about becoming parents.

Hannah donned her jacket and lifted her hand to wave as she exited the office.

I sighed as I shut down my computer.

I'd always wanted to experience everything Hannah had now.

A husband who loved me…

Making a life with a partner who accepted me exactly as I was…

Having a healthy child…

But since my life had spun out of control a year ago, none of those things even felt like a remote possibility for me anymore.

Chapter 2

Devon

I parked my truck in front of Glam Anywhere and glanced at my watch.

It was just after five, but I wanted to check on my pregnant sister-in-law because Tanner was going to be a little later than usual coming home today. He had a meeting that was running late with one of his companies, and he was still in the offices of Remington in Billings.

I didn't see Hannah's vehicle, and in a town this small, it wasn't like she had to find a parking spot far away from her office.

I could turn around and go home, figuring she had already left for the day.

However, I did see Reese's car, so I got my ass out of my truck.

Oh hell, who was I kidding?

I wasn't here to *just* check on Hannah.

Tanner hadn't asked me to stop by her office. He was going to call his wife as soon as the meeting ended to let her know he was headed home.

I just liked to tell myself that I was passing by to see how Hannah was doing.

In all honesty, I wanted to see if Hannah had mentioned my offer to teach Reese to ride this weekend.

I'd been completely unsuccessful in my quest to figure out who Reese Martin was and what she was really doing here in Crystal Fork.

I was hopeful that I could get more information out of her in a more relaxed setting.

What twenty-eight-year-old single woman moved to a town as small and isolated as Crystal Fork?

She was a beautiful, auburn-haired female with gorgeous, emerald-green eyes. Yet she was supposedly unattached?

There weren't many guys who wouldn't take a second and third look at Reese.

I'd probably find her attractive myself if I'd seen her walking down the street somewhere and if she wasn't a complete pain in my ass.

I grudgingly admitted that she also seemed intelligent and had a decent sense of humor when I wasn't throwing questions at her.

Strangely, it wasn't just facts that made me think something wasn't right with Reese.

For some reason, my gut had told me that since the beginning, and I'd never been able to shake those instincts.

I'd learned to listen to my intuition over the years in business. It had saved my ass a number of times.

And I couldn't ignore it when it came to Reese.

My gut was screaming at me that she wasn't being honest, and I was extremely fond of my sister-in-law.

On paper, the woman looked perfect.

She had a business degree and had never had any trouble with the law.

Not even a damn speeding or parking ticket.

Tanner thought I was being paranoid because he was really fond of Reese, and Hannah adored her.

However, I wasn't buying the image that was reflected in the bio I'd put together from her resume and public records.

Her body language and her adamant refusal to talk about herself told me everything I needed to know.

I was sure she got annoyed by all of my questions, but I didn't think that was why she avoided them.

It was something else that made her hesitant, and there was a glint of fear in those gorgeous green eyes of hers at times.

Reese Martin was a mystery I was determined to solve, and that determination was becoming an obsession.

She didn't have a criminal history, but whatever was up with Reese, I wanted to know exactly what she was hiding.

She was getting close to the people I cared about. Even my mother adored her, and I didn't want to see anyone hurt if this woman had secrets.

I might not always show it, but my family was everything to me.

When I entered Hannah's office, Reese was in the reception area.

She had her jacket on and was straightening up her desk like she was ready to leave.

The fact that she looked at me like she was definitely unhappy to see me was a hit to my ego, but I blew that off.

Reese always looked at me like I was a nasty bug that needed to be removed from the office immediately.

"I'm closing," she said flatly as she put a file away. "Hannah's not here. She went home a few minutes ago."

I ignored her not-so-subtle hint to leave.

Instead, I plopped my ass into a chair in front of her desk and got right to the point. "Did she mentioned that I offered to teach you to ride on Saturday?"

"Yes," she said in a clipped tone.

"And?" I prompted.

Her gaze finally met mine as she asked, "Why? We don't like each other and we're not exactly friends. We're not even friendly acquaintances."

I had to admit, the woman had spunk, and she spoke her mind.

I shrugged. "Why not? I have a bunch of horses that need the exercise. And I wouldn't say that I dislike you. I don't really know you well enough to make that kind of decision."

Yeah, that was a dig about her lack of openness, and she knew it.

She glared at me as she answered, "How much do you need to know about a stranger?"

"We'll always be strangers if we don't get to know each other."

"Are you telling me that you'd answer every question I asked you?" she asked in a more curious tone.

"I probably would," I said noncommittally. It depended on what she wanted to know. "Most of my past is common knowledge. I grew up here, and there aren't a lot of secrets in a small town."

"I'm just not like that, and I'm not used to it," she said in a genuine tone. "I lived in a busier place. Most people weren't interested in my life."

I had no doubt that her statement was honest. I hadn't exactly spilled every detail of my life to strangers when I'd lived in New York.

"I'm interested," I grumbled.

"Let's just be honest with each other about your motives for offering to teach me to ride," she said as she sat back down in her chair. "You want to pry more information out of me and seeing me outside of work provides you with a better atmosphere to do just that."

Shit! She was on to me.

I hadn't expected that.

Apparently, she was much more observant than I'd thought.

"Has it ever occurred to you that I just want to spend some time with you because you're a beautiful, intelligent woman?" I asked before I could stop myself.

That was not my real motive, but she was beautiful, and she was intelligent.

"Seriously?" she said with a snort. "I'm not your type."

I raised a brow. "What do you think is my type exactly?"

"I've heard that you don't really date. You mostly do hookups with women your age or older who don't want entanglements."

Living in a small town had its downsides, and people who gossiped was one of them. Reese had obviously heard about my preferences when it came to women.

I was going to have to convince her that I might want to change my ways. If she thought I was attracted to her, she might relax about me asking her so many questions. It *would* be better if she thought I was just interested in her because I liked her.

I couldn't say that I didn't realize that she was gorgeous but seriously pursuing her would never happen.

I didn't do serious relationships.

Especially not with a woman who was a decade younger than me.

"So you're the kind of woman who wants a husband and kids someday?" I asked cautiously.

She shrugged. "If I eventually meet the right man."

"Maybe I've just never met the right woman," I said nonchalantly.

To my chagrin, Reese rolled her eyes as she answered, "I doubt you've been looking for the right woman."

She was right, but I wasn't going to admit that to her.

I needed her to believe that I had some interest in her and wasn't just asking annoying questions because I was suspicious of her in some way.

It wasn't like she was going to be hurt if she realized that I wasn't smitten with her.

Reese definitely had no serious interest in me.

She'd made that perfectly clear.

I ignored her last comment and asked, "So are you going to learn to ride or not?"

She sighed unhappily. "I told Hannah I would. She thinks you're offering out of the goodness of your heart, and I didn't want to hurt her feelings. She wants to do something nice for me, and she can't teach me to ride when she's pregnant."

I grinned, genuinely amused because she sounded so forlorn about the whole idea.

I was a billionaire, fairly young to be so wealthy, and I wasn't horrible to look at. Most women pursued *me*.

I found it interesting that Reese would rather avoid me at all costs.

Still, I wasn't dissuaded.

I could be a charming guy when I wanted to be.

I'd just have to work a little harder to make Reese relax and actually enjoy my company.

She glanced at the clock. "I really need to close up. It's getting late."

I stood, finally taking her very obvious hint to get my ass out of the office.

"Hot date?" I teased.

She nodded. "A hot date with my wok in the kitchen. I love to cook. I'm trying out a new stir-fry dish I saw on a cooking show. After that, I'm going to binge watch some episodes of Antiques Roadshow. I missed a lot of episodes last season."

Okay, we were making progress. She'd actually shared a little information about herself.

Yeah, it was everyday information, but it was…something.

"I hate to cook," I admitted truthfully. "Can I come try out your new dish later?"

She laughed. "Do you want to watch Antiques Roadshow, too?" she joked.

She obviously thought I was joking.

"I saw all of last season's episodes, but I'll try not to spoil the surprises," I said hopefully.

I really wanted to finagle my way into her apartment. It might tell me more about her.

Plus, I really did hate to cook, but I loved to eat.

"No, you did not," she answered. "I don't see you as the kind of guy who watches collectibles and antiques shows."

"I've been collecting coins since I was a kid, but I also like to acquire rare items related to music. Rare musical instruments and vinyl records," I informed her. "I also collect art pieces that appeal to me. Mom is a huge fan of Antiques Roadshow, and she got me hooked years ago."

She sent me a skeptical look, like she couldn't figure out if I was for real.

"You're serious," she said as she looked me in the eyes. "I didn't see that coming."

I sent her one of my most charming smiles. "I like to surprise people. What time should I show up? Take pity on me, Reese. If you don't, I'll have to eat something frozen that I can toss in the microwave."

She frowned. "You know that stuff isn't healthy for you, especially if you eat it often. It's packed with sodium, saturated fats, and unhealthy additives."

She actually sounded concerned about my health, which caught me off-guard.

It was also kind of sweet, which was a word I never would have associated with Reese until this very moment.

I winked at her. "So are you going to save me from those terribly unhealthy things for one night?"

To be honest, I knew that my days of eating cardboard food for dinner should be ending. I was getting close to forty, but it never seemed to make sense to cook healthy food for myself. I usually didn't have the time, either. It was just easier to toss something into the microwave when I got home from my office in Billings.

I could only drop into my mom's place for dinner when I was getting home early, which wasn't that often. She'd been a rancher's wife for decades, so she went to bed early and was up at the crack of dawn.

Reese looked torn, like she was running her options over and over in her head.

It was kind of cute that she wanted to save me from myself, yet didn't want to spend time in my company.

"Seven-thirty," she finally said, sounding resigned.

So her empathy was stronger than her dislike of me?

That was intriguing.

And a little unsettling.

It told me that Reese was inherently a kind woman who put other's needs before her own.

If that was true, how dangerous could she possibly be to my family and the people I cared about?

"Wine?" I asked.

"I love it," she confessed. "But I don't drink it often. I usually prefer to eat my daily calories instead of drinking them.'

Apparently, she paid attention to what she ate and drank for health reasons, which I found a little surprising for a woman in her twenties who didn't appear to have a weight issue.

Reese was probably average height for a female.

She wasn't model thin, but she had her curves in all the right places.

"I'll bring a good German Reisling that I have in my wine cellar. I collect wines, too."

Her eyes lit up. "Then I'll make this one of those rare nights that I have a glass. I'm sure it's good wine."

"It's the best," I assured her as I walked toward the door.

"Do I want to know how expensive that wine is?" she called out before I left.

"Nope," I verified with a smirk. "Just consider it a thank you gift for feeding me."

I exited before she could change her mind about dinner.

As I got into my truck, I shook my head at the interesting turn of events that had just happened.

I was a cynical asshole, but Reese Martin had just surprised me.

In my world, that didn't happen very often, and strangely, it was kind of a pleasant surprise.

Chapter 3

Reese

What in the hell had I been thinking when I'd agreed to let Devon Remington come over for dinner?

I didn't like the guy.

His incessant questions had always been annoying.

He was supposedly a womanizer, and I knew he was cynical.

Yet, here I was, making dinner for both of us.

"I should have made a no questions rule part of the deal tonight," I muttered to myself as I cut up the vegetables for the stir-fry.

I still wasn't exactly sure why I'd relented and invited him to dinner.

Maybe, for just a moment, I'd wanted to believe that Devon wanted to be my friend. That he was interested in me as a person, which was why he was always asking questions.

I wanted to think that all of his motives weren't completely selfish.

I didn't think for a single moment that he wanted to date me or something like that.

From what I'd heard, his hookups were tall, thin, and very sophisticated.

I was none of those things.

I was barely average height at five-foot-four, and a little on the curvy side.

I loved food and cooking. I tried to keep it healthy most days because if I didn't, I would put on weight quickly. I liked to nourish my body with healthy food and stay away from chemical additives that were like poison to a body. However, I loved a good donut, ice cream, and carbs as much as the next woman. I was just careful about indulging in high calorie stuff more than was reasonable.

It had been a cold and pretty brutal winter, so I wasn't exercising as much as I normally did, and staying holed up in my apartment didn't help.

I definitely was not the type of woman Devon Remington would look at twice, but something had tugged at my heart when he'd said that he was going to go home and throw something out of a cardboard box into a microwave.

It had sounded like a lonely, unhealthy evening, and I'd always had kind of a caretaker personality.

It was probably ridiculous for me to feel sorry for a billionaire who had everything, but I'd sensed that Devon had really wanted to join me for dinner, and I'd instantly caved in.

Maybe I was just incredibly lonely myself, so I didn't want anyone to feel that way.

And I definitely didn't think he should be eating crappy food that wasn't good for him. The guy was pushing forty.

If he started in on the questions and the cynicism, I could always boot him out.

Was it possible that he really did want to get to know me?

Damn my curiosity! There was only one way to find out, and my relationships in Crystal Fork would be a lot better if I was on good terms with Devon and not always trying to avoid him.

I'd consider this evening a test to see if we could actually get along.

Obviously, we shared some common interests, and I really did want to learn to ride.

Truth was, I was bored out of my mind sometimes. I liked living in a small town, but I just wasn't used to not being occupied all the time.

In the city, I'd had friends over for dinner a lot, and I'd rarely had to eat alone.

I hadn't had sex or a serious relationship in years. Not since my last one had ended almost four years ago, but I'd had a ton of good friends and my parents to keep me company.

Yeah, I'd dated a little, but I'd just never found anyone I'd connected with in years.

I was developing friendships here in Crystal Fork. I had Hannah, Lauren, and Anna, but they had their own lives here. Husbands. Family. Other friends. Lauren was my only single friend, but she had connections here that were like family to her.

As Hannah had said, they'd all invited me to go to Billings and for other outings, but if it involved going out of the area, I just couldn't do it.

Honestly, I probably shouldn't let myself get too close to anyone in Crystal Fork, but I loved people, and I liked having friends.

I didn't think there was any harm in trying to have a good relationship with Devon if that was possible.

I liked and respected Kaleb and Tanner, and it would be far easier if I didn't dislike their younger brother.

I was also really fond of Millie Remington, their mother, and it was hard to skirt around the topic of Devon all the time because I had nothing good to say about that particular Remington.

Maybe I was just paranoid about his motivations.

I was pretty wary of almost everyone right now.

Hannah had said that she hoped I could see the other side of Devon.

I guess I was hoping for the same thing.

Today, Devon had intrigued me even more because he'd actually been sort of…nice.

If he had been his normal growly self and pestering me with question after question, I wouldn't be here making dinner for both of us.

I also had to admit that even though Devon was pegged as a womanizer, I'd actually never seen him with a woman in Crystal Fork. He was normally with his brothers, his mother, or friends. I had no doubt that he had his share of women, but he obviously didn't bring them home to Crystal Fork.

Woman had to be falling all over him. He was ridiculously hot with a droolworthy, muscular body. His enormous wealth and power also probably made him a magnet for women who wanted a remarkably successful man.

Yet, if the rumors about him were true, he'd never had a real, committed, serious relationship. Everyone around town said he just had brief flings with women who looked and acted like supermodels.

It was obviously Devon's choice to stay a bachelor with no romantic attachments.

Part of me really wondered why.

There was nothing wrong with not wanting a relationship, but there was usually some reason for making that choice.

Had he really never met the right woman, or did he avoid entanglements because he had a reason for avoiding relationships?

It was really none of my business, but I'd found myself wondering about that a lot over the last few hours.

I sighed as I finished preparing the meat and vegetables and went to wash my hands.

I'd ended up stopping at the local market to get things for a quick dessert, something I hadn't planned on before Devon invited himself to dinner.

I was doing stuffed baked apples with cinnamon, raisins, and nuts because it was easy. They had a little brown sugar, but it was healthier than most desserts.

They were cored and stuffed. I'd put them into the oven before we ate dinner.

The doorbell rang as I was drying my hands, and a glance at my watch told me that Devon was right on time.

I'd showered and changed into a pair of nice jeans and a green, cropped sweater.

I smiled as I went to the door, knowing my outfit was a step up from my usual attire in the evenings, which consisted of baggy sweatpants and an oversized T-shirt.

Since I was always alone, I went for the most comfortable clothes I could find in my closet.

I opened the door to find Devon similarly dressed and grinning at me in an ivory, cable-knit sweater, and jeans.

My breath caught for just a moment.

I generally didn't see him in a casual outfit. He always stopped into the office in a custom suit because he was coming from the office, and he was *never* smiling.

The ivory color of the sweater contrasted stunningly with his dark coloring, and that devilish grin of his just…got to me.

You have to stop noticing how attractive he is, Reese. Stop it right now!

I couldn't let this man get to me in any way.

Devon Remington was nothing more than a hostile acquaintance that I wanted to be more comfortable with.

He was my boss's brother-in-law for God's sake.

I *had* to be immune to his good looks and his charm.

That wasn't an easy thing to do when he was eying me from head to toe as he commented huskily, "Your sweater matches your eyes."

It wasn't a cheesy line. Coming from Devon, it was just an observation, but said in that sexy baritone of his, it sounded like…seduction.

Hell, almost anything he said with that cocky grin on his face would sound sexy.

I laughed as I held the door open for him. "I didn't do it intentionally. I just liked the color."

Devon closed and locked the apartment door behind him and followed me into the small kitchen. "I'll put the wine in the fridge," he said as he did just that. "What can I do to help?"

"Nothing," I said as I started to prepare the stir-fry. "Everything is ready. I'll have it ready in minutes. I'd give you a tour of my place, but you can see most of it from the kitchen."

"I'm assuming it's the same as Hannah's," he said conversationally. "I was there a few times."

Devon had already known that I'd lived in the same building as Hannah had, but he'd texted me to confirm the apartment.

My guess was that he'd gotten my number from Hannah.

"Exactly the same," I confirmed. "It's small, but it's cozy."

Devon wandered into the living room before he said, "I see that you decorate with some of your antique finds."

"It's a little eclectic," I told him as he walked back into the kitchen. "Some older, some newer. I've never been lucky enough to find anything or buy anything that's really expensive, but I love to go to thrift stores and antique shops looking for treasures. Nothing I've ever gotten is extremely valuable. I just buy the pieces that speak to me in some way. Furniture. Jewelry. Books. Art. I buy a little of everything."

He shot me a curious look as he rested his hip against the entry to the kitchen. "How does it speak to you? And I like your style. It's unique."

I added spices to the veggies and chicken as I answered, "Thanks. I can't really explain it. Sometimes I'm just drawn to certain things." I paused before I asked, "Are you okay with spice?"

"The spicier the better," he confirmed. "The local food in Thailand and India are a few of my favorites, and it's definitely not the Americanized versions we get here."

"I've never been to either country, but I'd like to get there one day," I said with a sigh as I added a little more spice. I was with him on the spice level. I liked my stir-fry hot. "You're probably incredibly well traveled."

"Not as much as I'd like to be," he replied. "But yeah, I've been to a lot of different countries. I'm usually there on business, but I try to incorporate those visits with some sightseeing. What about you?"

It didn't feel like he was trying to pry into my personal life with his question, so I told him, "Only a few trips on vacation so far. Canada, Mexico, The Bahamas, and England. I was busy with work and college. My goal is to explore more of the world as soon as possible. Sometimes life just gets in the way."

"Dream vacation?" he asked.

I answered instantly. "I want to go to The Galapagos Islands. There are species there that don't exist anywhere else in the world, and it was Darwin's inspiration for his theory of evolution. Greece is a close second because of the historical significance, and Egypt for the same reason."

Devon's eyes widened. "That isn't exactly what I expected you to say. I've been to Greece, but Galapagos and Egypt are pretty high on my list of places I'd like to visit, too. They're not exactly places where I have business to do. I take it you're not the type of woman who wants to lie on the beach and relax."

"I like the beach. I love to swim, but my fair skin burns pretty easily, and I don't want to fry all day. It's boring," I informed him. "If I have free time, I want to explore and learn something."

He crossed his muscular arms over his chest and just observed me for a minute like he'd never seen me before.

The silence was just getting uncomfortable when he drawled, "You're an interesting woman, Reese Martin. I think I'm going to enjoy getting to know you better."

I sent him a hesitant smile because my heart ached just a little.

I was starting to think I'd like to get to know Devon, too, but he'd never really be able to get to know me.

There were parts of me he could never know.

I could tell him my likes and dislikes, but it was impossible for him to know everything about me.

And for the first time since I'd known Devon, I was starting to regret that fact.

Chapter 4

Devon

"Dinner was incredible," I told Reese as we enjoyed a glass of wine in the living room after dinner.

I wasn't trying to flatter her.

She *was* an amazing cook, and she'd fed me until I couldn't eat another bite, which was unusual for me since I had an extremely healthy appetite.

The stir-fry had been some of the tastiest I'd ever had, and I'd never known that stuffed apples could be that good.

I couldn't say that I'd learned a lot about her from being in her apartment except that she'd been telling the truth about her love for cooking.

She'd obviously brought a few things with her when she'd moved, like the smattering of vintage items I'd seen scattered around her living room.

I'd only seen one large photo on a tiny vintage table along the wall. She'd told me it was her favorite picture of her parents.

Otherwise…nothing that really said anything significant about her past.

Reese's apartment was so small that she didn't have a table, so we had eaten on TV trays in her living room.

She was obviously getting comfortable with me because we'd talked a lot throughout our dinner.

She didn't seem hesitant to answer my questions, but I was a lot more subtle, asking less invasive getting-to-know-her questions.

I wasn't grilling her like I used to, and I found myself interested in her answers simply because she was a fascinating woman.

Just like her decorating, her interests were eclectic, and she was knowledgeable on more subjects than I'd expected.

I'd discovered that she loved to read everything from nonfiction to romance, so that might be where she acquired her knowledge.

She was incredibly intelligent, even more so than I'd thought earlier.

I was starting to find myself asking questions about things I didn't need to know simply because I was intrigued by the way her mind worked.

How was it possible that I'd known Reese for months, but had never realized that she was probably a woman I could actually like?

Hell, that was probably my fault because I'd put her on the defensive almost immediately.

The only problem I had with spending time in Reese's company was that my dick was starting to like her, too.

Every damn time she laughed or smiled at me, my cock responded instantly.

I'd always known she was beautiful.

I knew a lot of beautiful women.

But the more that I got to know Reese, the more attractive she became to me.

I was trying to avoid getting close to her physically because she smelled like citrus and vanilla. It was a pleasant scent, and it definitely shouldn't be seductive, but it was for me.

That was a problem, and something I needed to get a grip on right now.

I just wished that my body and mind were in agreement.

I watched as her tongue darted out to delicately lick her lips after a sip of her wine.

B. A. Scott

Christ! I wanted nothing more than to conquer those lips myself, and a guy could have fantastic fantasies about that tongue and where he wanted it on his body.

Right. Fucking. Now.

Put a lid on it, Remington. Not going to happen!

I tried to remember why I was really here with Reese, but over the course of the last two hours, the lines were starting to get a little blurry for me.

"Are you okay?" Reese asked softly. "You got quiet. Was the food too spicy? I could get you an antacid if you need it."

I held up a hand. "I'm good. I was just thinking about that great food and savoring a good glass of wine."

And I was a major liar, which I hated.

In reality, I was fantasizing about all of the things I could do to her curvy body if I could just get her naked.

I also wanted to know *all* of her secrets now, and not just to protect my family.

For some damn reason, I wanted to protect Reese, too.

I sensed a vulnerability in her that concerned me, and my instinct *was* to protect her.

She was being a little more forthcoming, but that quick glint of fear in her eyes I saw occasionally was very real.

She hid it well, and it was probably something most people would never notice, but I could sense it as well.

If I hit on a topic she didn't want to talk about, I could literally feel her hesitation, even though she covered it up almost immediately.

What in the hell was going on with Reese Martin, and why in the hell did I give a shit about the possibility of hitting on a topic that scared her?

How had she gone from a possible threat to someone I wanted to protect in a matter of hours?

She very well could be lying to all of us, but instead of that pissing me off like it used to, I found myself asking why she'd do something like that.

Everyone had a past.

Past heartache.

Past mistakes.

Things that had happened in the past that we regretted.

No one who liked her was going to judge her for that.

Had some asshole broken her heart and she was here in Montana to escape that heartache?

That theory just didn't ring true to me unless he was still a threat to her in some way.

My gut told me that Reese wasn't the type to dump her entire life in the city to escape heartache in rural Montana.

"Thank you for offering to teach me to ride," she said. "I'm sorry now that I accused you of having ulterior motives."

Okay, now I felt guilty, and that almost never happened.

I did have ulterior motives, and her comment made me feel like a prick.

Wanting to distract myself, I questioned, "Any idea what kind of horse you want to learn to ride on? Any fears about riding?"

She shook her head. "I'm not sure. I'm excited. My only experience with riding is being led around on a pony as a kid. I guess my only fear is getting on a gigantic horse and being so high off the ground. You're the teacher. I'll be happy to take whatever horse you suggest. Do you have a lot of horses?"

I nodded. "Quite a few. I think I'd put you on Luna. She's a Gypsy Vanner horse. A beautiful tobiano black and white from champion lines. She was Mom's horse, but she had to scale down her riding to one horse because of her arthritis, so I took Luna. She has a sweet disposition and she's not very intimidating. It's a short breed in general, but they're muscular and strong. I think you two would be perfect for each other, and she doesn't get enough exercise. She's a little too small for me and my barn manager, so Lauren exercises her for me when she can. She also exercises Mom's horse that she still has at the ranch when my mother isn't able to ride."

Reese smiled. "I can help. Once I can ride, I'd help your mom out when she needs it and exercise Luna every day for you. It's the least I can do to pay you back for teaching me to ride. I know Lauren gets busy when she's on an important project, and she favors one of Tanner's horses."

"She does," I confirmed. "She exercises Mom's horse and Luna as a favor. Tanner gave her the horse she likes to ride, and they have a bond. What happens if you end up hating to ride?"

"I won't," she said confidently. "I've always been an animal lover. I've just never had the opportunity to learn to ride a horse."

"Come early on Saturday," I instructed. "We'll go over some safety stuff and the basics of riding before I get you on Luna. You said you liked to swim. Bring a suit. I have an indoor pool and a hot tub. You might want to soak for a while. You'll be sore when you first start riding."

"Are you saying that my butt is going to hurt?" she said jokingly.

"Pretty much," I responded, trying not to think about her gorgeous ass that I'd be more than willing to massage for her after her ride. "Unless you exercise your glutes and all of the other muscles you need to ride, you'll be sore. Sitting on a horse in the same position stretches muscles you didn't know you had."

"I don't get the exercise I used to," she said wistfully. "There's no gym here, and Montana is way too cold for a winter walk. Now that it's getting warmer, I'll be able to get outdoors more. I love to walk and take hikes, but not when it's as cold as it's been over the winter."

I nodded. "That's why I have an indoor pool and a gym."

She laughed, and the musical sound made my gut ache. "I don't think I'm fitting any exercise equipment into this apartment," she joked. "I thought about an exercise bike or a treadmill, but I'm not sure where I'd put it."

She was right. There was barely room for furniture, and if her bedroom looked like Hannah's had, it was barely big enough for a decent sized bed and a dresser.

"Have you always had a place this small?" I asked curiously. "I think I'd go crazy if I was confined to this small of a space in the winter."

She hesitated for a second before she answered, "No. But I really don't mind this place being small. It's just me here. I don't have to waste a lot of time cleaning, and it feels…safer. I wish the kitchen was a little bigger, but I don't have a lot of choice of apartments in Crystal Fork. They're all pretty small, and there really aren't any rental homes here. Most people own and live in their homes."

The fact that she mentioned feeling safer here didn't escape me, but I got the feeling I shouldn't push her on that comment right now.

I was going to have to let her keep some of her secrets until she felt comfortable enough to share.

I'd make the mistake of grilling her about her former life once, and that had pushed her away.

I tried to be a guy who never did stupid things more than once.

"Nobody really rents homes here," I agreed. "We're not exactly high on the list of tourist destinations in Montana. If you ever want to use my pool or my gym, feel free."

She shook her head. "I'd never intrude on you like that, and I'm not sure that I should overstay my welcome on Saturday. I'm sure you're a busy guy, and you're already taking the time out of your weekend to teach me to ride."

I shrugged. "Everyone helps each other here. We don't consider helping other people in town an inconvenience. I have a big place. I'd never even know you were there."

She looked a little flustered as she asked, "What if you have… company? That would be a little awkward."

I grinned at her. "Are you asking if I have wild orgies at my house every night?"

"I didn't mean *that*," she said as she sent me a scolding look that was kind of adorable. "But you must date sometimes. You're a single guy."

"I don't bring dates back to Crystal Fork," I replied, amused. "None of my previous dates would have any interest in hanging out here, and I'd never date anyone here."

Honestly, I didn't really date at all.

Yeah, I'd had two women that I'd hooked up with occasionally in Billings and Bozeman. Like me, they hadn't wanted any romantic entanglement.

Eventually, we'd just gone our separate ways.

One of them had ended up in a committed relationship even though she'd always sworn that it was never going to happen, and the other had moved to New York.

Truth was, it had been a while since I'd gotten laid, but it hadn't bothered me enough to seek out another arrangement.

The rumors about me being some kind of a playboy were highly inflated.

I was no angel. I'd had a few brief flings in my travels, too, but I hadn't done that in a long time.

My sex drive was still healthy, but those experiences were kind of empty and pointless once the sex part of it was over.

Maybe I'd grown up and realized that there was more to life than getting laid every single night.

My attraction to Reese had surprised me.

I hadn't felt this attracted to a woman in a long time, and it was disconcerting that it just happened to be a woman who was completely off-limits.

"Why would you never date someone who lived here?" Reese asked curiously.

"Not happening," I grumbled. "I've known most of the single women here since we were kids. We've been friends forever. There actually aren't a lot of single women here that are my age."

I had to remind myself not to tell her that almost every single female in Crystal Fork wanted a commitment, marriage, and kids.

If I wanted Reese to think that I hadn't settled down because I'd never met the right woman, that wasn't a comment I wanted to come out of my mouth right now.

"Just bring your suit and a change of clothes on Saturday," I added. "You're definitely not going to be running into any company at my place. Spending time with you is something I want to do, Reese. It's not an inconvenience."

She worried her bottom lip with her teeth as she looked at me like she was trying to figure me out.

Fuck! I knew she still didn't trust me, and that bugged the shit out of me for some reason.

She was actually a smart woman, and probably right not to trust me since I wasn't exactly being honest with her, either.

I hated the relief I felt when she finally nodded slowly in agreement.

I also hated the fact that I wasn't sure if I was relieved because I wanted to pry information out of her or if I just wanted to spend the day with *her*.

Today was Thursday.

I had two days to get my priorities straight and my dick in check so I could focus on my real objective.

I *would* get over this attraction to Reese, and I'd definitely get the information I wanted.

Chapter 5

Reese

"I heard that you had dinner with Devon at your place last night," Anna said in a teasing voice as we had lunch with Lauren and Hannah the next day at Charlie's.

I really liked Anna, but I still wasn't quite used to seeing her over a lunch table in rural Montana.

She was one of the most famous pop stars on the planet, and the adjustments she'd had to make to marry Kaleb and live here with him in Crystal Fork hadn't been easy.

Strangely, she seemed to love it here, and she seemed incredibly happy.

She had to go out of town fairly often for appearances, but she wasn't doing big tours anymore, which she'd told me had completely burned her out anyway.

It was pretty apparent to me that she and Kaleb belonged together, and she fit right into the town and was embraced as one of their own.

It didn't hurt that Kaleb had a private jet that would wing her away to any of her appearances.

He joined her as often as possible, and it was pretty sweet that he got a little testy when she was away, and he couldn't be with her.

Her recording studio in Billings was completed and she was currently using it to record her next album release.

My brows rose as I stared at Anna. "How did you hear that?"

"I heard it, too." Lauren said from her seat beside Anna.

"I heard it early this morning from my mother, but I'd already figured something was up when Devon asked me for your phone number last night," Hannah joined in from beside me. "Surely you don't think that you could do something like that quietly in this town. Juicy gossip spreads like a wildfire here. Everyone knows Devon's truck and his other vehicles, and the neighbors were paying attention when he walked up to your door."

"How was the date?" Lauren said excitedly. "Devon has never dated anyone here, so I'm dying to know."

I shook my head as I swallowed a bite of my salad so I could speak. "It was not a date," I said emphatically. "He stopped by the office late, and he mentioned that he was eating cardboard food. He invited himself to dinner and I fed him because I didn't want him to have to eat nasty food. It was completely innocent. End of story."

"I personally think he likes you," Hannah commented after she polished off her sandwich. "He's at my office every day when he can get off work in time to pass by."

"He wants to check up on me," I told her drily. "He's still trying to figure out why I'm here in Crystal Fork and why I left the city to take this job."

Anna sent me a quizzical look. "Did it ever occur to you that he might just want to get to know you?"

I hesitated before I answered. "No. Until yesterday, he was almost hostile toward me. He treated me like the enemy. I'm not quite sure what happened, but he's suddenly being…nice."

Too nice!

I wished that I could figure out why he was suddenly so different.

The change in Devon was confusing, and it had thrown me off-balance.

It wasn't exactly unwelcome, but after so many months of him antagonizing me, I had no idea what to think about him anymore.

I wanted to believe that this was the other side of Devon that everyone talked about, but it had happened so abruptly that I couldn't be completely sure that he was sincere.

Hannah snorted. "Devon is hostile and careful with everyone until he gets to know them. Once he trusts you, he lightens up."

"Devon and I bonded over music," Anna mentioned. "But I can't say he was that open about anything else until I'd known him for a while."

"I know he plays because he filled in for some band member at The Mug And Jug one night," I mused. "But I didn't get a chance to see him perform."

Anna nodded. "He usually does that on the guitar, but Devon is a musical genius. Much more talented than I am. There aren't many instruments he can't play, and he's better than I am on the piano, too. He collaborates with me on writing some of my songs, but he'll never take credit for that. Give him some time, Reese. He'll grow on you. He really is a nice guy."

The problem was, Devon was *already* starting to grow on me. I'd seen a much nicer, more interesting side of him yesterday.

Unfortunately, he could also be very charming when he chose to be, and I was seeing a much more attractive side of him.

"He invited me to stay and use his pool and his hot tub after my riding lesson," I shared.

Lauren sighed. "Do it. He has the most amazing pool, and his hot tub is big enough to have a party in. I've gone there to use them both over the winter." She paused before she said, "You don't look excited about his offer. Are you afraid he's going to turn into the grouchy Devon again?"

So he let Lauren use his pool and gym?

Maybe offering to let people use the space was something he did on a regular basis.

He'd obviously been sincere in his offer to let me use it any time I wanted.

I wasn't afraid he was suddenly going to do an about-face on me and turn back into the grumpy Devon again.

Not really.

I hadn't seen a single sign of the old Devon last night, and it was probably unlikely that he was suddenly going to change...again.

But I wasn't sure that spending more time with Devon than necessary was a great idea.

I was starting to feel weirdly attracted to him, and that scared me.

Devon was a devastatingly attractive guy, but I'd never wanted to get him naked until yesterday.

God, I hadn't even liked the man before our dinner last night.

I certainly hadn't had sexual fantasies about him in the past.

"He's not going to change," Anna assured me.

"How do you know that?" I asked her curiously.

"Devon is kind of like the people of Crystal Fork. Once he sees you as one of his own, he's protective. He's a little less obvious than his brothers, but that man has a protective streak a mile long."

I put my fork down on my empty plate as I asked, "Can I ask a nosy question?"

"Yes!"

"Absolutely!"

"We love nosy questions!"

I smiled at the women at the table, and I was so glad that I could call them all my friends.

"It's probably none of my business," I started hesitantly. "But are all the stories about him being a player true?"

Hannah opened her mouth to speak first. "It's a lot of exaggeration," she explained. "I've known Devon for a long time. When we were all living in New York, I think he got laid occasionally, but he was never interested in a relationship. For the first year or two after he moved there, I don't think he saw anyone at all. Not even for a hookup. The man is thirty-eight years old, and he's never been in a meaningful relationship. I suspect that he got burned really badly at some point when he was in college, but he blows us off if we ask what happened. He's never even mentioned what happened to Kaleb or Tanner."

I digested that information for a moment before I replied, "Maybe he's just not a relationship kind of guy."

Hannah shook her head. "I don't think that's true. He has a lot to give to the people he cares about. I don't think he loves being alone. I just don't think he's met the right woman. It would definitely have to be someone who could gain his trust completely."

Lauren gave me an inquisitive look. "Are you interested in Devon? You'd be perfect for him."

"No!" I said emphatically. "I'm not his type, and we disliked each other until yesterday."

"Why couldn't you be his type?" Anna questioned. "You're beautiful and highly intelligent. Lauren's right. You'd never put up with too much of his bullshit, and that would be good for him."

"I've heard that his past women have been tall, thin, stunningly gorgeous, and sophisticated. I'm none of those things. I'm also very boring. My idea of excitement is cooking, reading a good book, or searching for antiques."

"Devon isn't exactly a party animal," Anna pointed out. "He spends a lot of time in his music room, reading, and hanging out with people he likes. He goes to The Mug And Jug occasionally, but he's kind of a loner most of the time. He has hooked up with a few supermodels for a fling, but people make a bigger deal out of that than they should. It was a long time ago, and there was nothing there but a very brief physical attraction. I really don't think he has a type. He's never really had a girlfriend."

"Just keep an open mind," Hannah suggested. "I still think he has a thing for you. Are you really not interested in him?"

"It would never happen," I said firmly. "I guess I'm just hoping we can be…friendlier."

If Devon needed someone he could trust completely that woman could *never* be me. I'd been lying to the people here in Crystal Fork from day one.

He'd most likely hate me if he ever found out the truth.

"Give him a chance tomorrow to show you a different side of himself," Hannah requested. "Relax and just have fun. His property is gorgeous and there are endless trails to ride. Tanner made multiple mountain bike trails that run through his, Kaleb's, and Devon's properties. We use them for the horses, too."

I knew the three brothers had connecting properties, and that they all had a significant amount of acreage.

My eyes widened. "That's a lot of property and trails."

"A ridiculous amount," Hannah agreed.

I glanced at my watch and realized how long we'd been gone from the office. "I'd better get back to work. My lunch hour was over a while ago."

Hannah laughed. "It's Friday. We deserve a long lunch. The three of us aren't available to get together very often."

"We're going into Billings on Sunday to do some shopping and then get something to eat," Anna said enthusiastically. "Are you coming with us?"

God, probably none of them had any idea how badly I wanted to go with them.

I craved the company and the friendship these women were offering me, but I knew I couldn't.

"I'm sorry. I can't. I have other plans. Maybe next time." I finally forced those words out of my mouth even though my heart was aching.

"You always say that," Hannah grumbled unhappily.

She was right, and I was getting damn tired of saying no, but as of right now, there was no other answer I could give them.

Chapter 6

Devon

"I heard you're starting Reese's riding lessons tomorrow," Tanner said as he and Kaleb sat in my office at Remington Friday afternoon.

We'd just finished going over some business we had to resolve before the weekend.

"That's the plan," I said nonchalantly.

"What prompted you to do that?" Kaleb asked with curiosity in his voice. "I thought you two didn't really get along. And then I heard this morning that you were at her house last night. Are you still trying to get information about her previous life out of her?"

I shot a disgruntled look at my brother from behind my desk. Of course he'd heard that I was at Reese's house the night before. Gossip spread quickly in Crystal Fork. "I know you both think I'm crazy, but there's something that's just not sitting well with me about her."

Tanner let out a beleaguered breath before he spoke. "Look, you've been saying that almost since she got here. There's nothing weird going on. She's been a valuable employee and friend to Hannah, and I happen to like her, too. I haven't seen anything strange with the business, and I go over Hannah's business account with her. We did a thorough background check. What in the hell still makes you think that something's not right with Reese? I think you're paranoid. She's not a criminal hiding out in Crystal Fork, Devon. She's a nice woman."

"Anna and I really like her, too," Kaleb added. "And Mom and Lauren adore her."

"I'm not saying she's a damn criminal," I grumbled. "I just said that something's not right. I know I have no tangible evidence of that, but my gut won't leave it alone. I don't think she's left Crystal Fork since she got here. She's an attractive, single woman. Wouldn't you think she'd go to Billings or Bozeman to the clubs once in a while? Or meet someone from there on dating apps or something?"

Kaleb lifted a brow. "You're a single guy. Do you do that? Are you on dating apps meeting women in those cities? Maybe she's sick of the bar scene and dating apps."

"Okay," I replied readily. "But what about shopping and other activities you can't find in Crystal Fork? Tell me your wives aren't in Billings at least once a month to get something they can't get here."

"Sometimes more," Tanner agreed. "And I can bring Hannah whatever she wants since our offices are here. She's had a lot of cravings for things that I can't get in Crystal Fork lately."

I watched Tanner's face, but there wasn't a single sign that Hannah's needs during her pregnancy annoyed him. In fact, he was grinning.

I knew that he'd bend over backwards to get Hannah whatever she wanted.

Most of the time, he was anticipating his wife's wants and needs before she ever said a word.

My older brother had been a different person since he'd married Hannah.

He was…happy.

Happy in a way he hadn't been since she'd walked out of his life years ago.

He had no idea how much I'd wanted that for him.

I'd wanted the same for Kaleb, and my eldest brother had found the woman he was meant to spend his life with in Anna.

Married life wasn't for me, but I'd always known my brothers weren't meant to live their lives alone.

I was going to be an uncle, and that seemed almost unbelievable to me.

I could only imagine how Tanner felt knowing he was going to be a father soon.

"Anna is starting to think about kids," Kaleb shared.

"And?" I asked, already knowing that Kaleb would love to be a father.

He shot me a lopsided grin. "I'm more than ready to do my part in getting her pregnant. Hell, I'd love to see her pregnant with my child, but it will definitely screw up her career for a while. She's still traveling a lot, even though she records her music in her studio in Billings. I don't want her to make sacrifices for me. I love her. Just having her as my wife is enough."

I shook my head slowly. "I don't think it would be a sacrifice for her. She wants to have kids, right?"

He nodded. "Hopefully more than one, which is why she's thinking about getting started soon. She's going to start slowly decreasing her traveling and personal appearances. She keeps saying that she's not getting any younger."

Tanner barked out a laugh. "Hannah says the same thing, but this pregnancy thing scares the shit out of me. Well, not really the pregnancy, but the labor and the discomfort Hannah is going to go through to bring our kid into the world. Once I watch the pain she'll go through during the birth, I'm not sure I can do it again. And anything could happen during childbirth."

"Nothing bad is going to happen," I assured Tanner. "Women have babies every day. Hannah will be fine."

"She'll have to be," Tanner answered in a disgruntled voice. "Hannah is my entire world now."

Kaleb nodded like he understood completely. "Just like Anna is mine."

I couldn't say that I related to what they were saying because I didn't believe that one person could be your entire world, but I knew my brothers.

If anything happened to their wives, neither one of them would ever be the same.

I could comprehend that much, which is why I tried to watch out for them.

Truthfully, Hannah and Anna were family to me now, and I'd do anything to keep them safe.

My concern about Reese had all started because of my protective instincts for my family.

"I still plan on figuring out what's going on with Reese," I warned them. "Maybe she'll tell me more if we're on friendlier terms."

"Don't push on her, Devon," Tanner warned. "She seems like a private person, and we all should respect that. She wasn't raised here in Crystal Fork where everyone trusts their neighbors. We all grew up here. She's still adjusting."

"I'm not sure she's just trying to be private. I think she's scared," I finally blurted out.

A look of concern formed on my brothers' faces.

"What makes you think that?" Tanner asked.

"Fuck!" I cursed, feeling frustrated. "Gut instinct. The flash of fear I see in her eyes for just a nanosecond before she masks it. She'll share some things with me easily. Her likes. Her dislikes. Some of her past experiences. But when it comes to specifics about her past, she clams up like she's afraid to say anything."

"I guess I can't give you any input about that," Tanner admitted. "I've never felt the need to interrogate her on her background. However, there's something to be said about your gut instinct. You're almost never wrong."

I hadn't always had a good gut instinct.

I wished that I'd been born with it, but I'd developed it and listened to it as I'd matured.

"I did notice that she's friendly with Chief Norton," Kaleb mentioned. "Anna and I saw them having coffee at Charlie's a while back. But Norton makes it a point to know everyone in this town. He's been reacquainting himself with everyone and meeting the townspeople he doesn't know."

Ralph Norton was our Chief of Police. He'd been hired and had started his position not long before Reese had moved here.

Kaleb had made it a point to improve our police department after our cousin, Shelby, had been kidnapped and almost killed by a serial killer while she was staying in Crystal Fork.

Ralph Norton was single, but a lot older than Reese. About thirty years older. Unless Reese was really into much older men, I doubted there was any romantic interest there on either side.

Kaleb had helped recruit Norton from Spokane, where he'd been known as a very experienced and very savvy senior detective.

Originally from Crystal Fork, Ralph had fit right back into the town like he'd never been gone for a few decades.

"He's met with a lot of the residents at some point," Tanner pointed out. "Hannah and I had dinner with him a few months ago."

"Same here," Kaleb agreed. "I think he's just a friendly guy who wants to connect with his town again. I never really thought it was unusual."

I frowned. "Maybe she just wants to make sure she's comfortable with the law enforcement here."

Crystal Fork had never had much of a police force, but all of that had changed after Shelby was kidnapped. The person in charge at the time had very little experience with serious crimes and didn't know a thing about the procedures involved in a kidnapping.

My cousin had nearly died because the proper procedures hadn't been followed, and Kaleb had been like a bulldog about fixing that issue.

We all had.

We'd all been more than willing to make a big enough donation every year to pay for a decent police force.

"Now you really are being paranoid," Tanner drawled. "Are you sure that you're only concerned about your family's welfare and not Reese's safety?"

"What if some asshole is stalking her?" I questioned. "It makes sense. Maybe she moved here to get away from a former boyfriend."

"Why don't you just ask her if you're worried about her," Tanner questioned. "You ask her about everything else."

"Too personal," I informed him. "I've decided that I need her to trust me to tell me anything that personal about herself."

"It's going to be hard for her to trust you when you have ulterior motives for teaching her to ride," Kaleb said drily.

"Or is all of that bullshit?" Tanner questioned suspiciously. "Why do I have a feeling you're starting to like her and want to spend time with her?"

I didn't.

My dick was apparently starting to adore her, which was exactly why I *shouldn't* spend time with her.

"She's smart," I conceded. "And we have a few things in common. Maybe I could like her if she wasn't hiding things."

"She's also a beautiful woman," Kaleb said.

"She's a decade younger than I am, and she's not my type," I assured him.

The last thing I needed was my brothers to start playing matchmaker.

I wasn't a guy who had a match out there somewhere like they did.

They knew that I didn't do committed relationships.

Hell, my brothers had never tried to fix me up with anyone before.

I hoped that wasn't going to change now that they were happily married and possibly thought I should be, too.

"Does ten years really mean anything now that you're older? Reese is pretty mature," Tanner said offhandedly as he held up his palm. "Not that I'm trying to encourage any kind of relationship with Reese. You've never committed to a woman in your life, and if you hurt her, I'd be pissed."

"Someday you're going to have to tell us what happened to make you such a prick when it comes to women," Kaleb insisted.

Oh, hell no, that was not going to happen in this lifetime. "It's just the way I am," I answered. "Not everyone *wants* a committed relationship."

"I didn't want one either before I met Anna," Kaleb shot back. "Someday, some woman is going to knock you on your ass."

"It hasn't happened in thirty-eight years," I replied drily. "It's not going to happen."

"Just be nice to Reese tomorrow," Tanner said firmly. "She really wants to learn to ride, and you might actually enjoy her company if you let yourself."

I didn't make a smartass comment, which was my normal.

Maybe because he was right.

I probably could enjoy her company if I let myself, but I didn't plan to let my guard down long enough to find out.

I was too fucking attracted to her, and that was going to have to keep me on the defensive the whole damn day.

I watched as Tanner stood, telling us that he had to pick up something for Hannah and then he was headed home.

Kaleb followed.

I stayed in my office longer than I'd planned, trying to plan exactly how I could get closer to Reese and keep my defenses completely intact.

Chapter 7

Reese

I heard music the moment I walked through the door of Devon's home Saturday morning.

He was on the piano playing what sounded like a beautiful but complicated jazz piece.

I'd had a text from Devon when I'd woken up this morning telling me to just let myself in because the door would be unlocked. He'd mentioned that he'd be in his music room and might not hear the doorbell.

I shook my head as I juggled the items I was carrying and closed the door gently with my foot.

It was still hard to get used to people leaving their doors unlocked, but that was the way things worked here in Crystal Fork.

I certainly didn't do it.

My door got locked the moment I closed it, and that wasn't going to change for me anytime soon.

I looked around the home as soon as I entered. It was a very open floorplan with lofty ceilings, so it wasn't hard to spot the kitchen.

Devon's home wasn't just a home, it was a mansion, but somehow he'd still managed to keep it warm and welcoming. I'd felt it the moment I'd seen the exterior after driving down the long driveway.

It didn't look like a showpiece that was meant to impress people, but it was still pretty impressive.

It was just…gigantic.

I took in the beautiful artwork on the walls as I made my way to the kitchen, one in particular that I suspected was a work by his mother. Millie had a very distinctive style.

I had to hold back an audible gasp as I entered Devon's kitchen.

For anyone who loved to cook, it was a dream kitchen.

For a man who only used the microwave, it was funny how he'd managed to have every high-end toy and gadget any chef would love.

I opened his fridge to put in the things I'd brought and noticed that he had very little in the enormous space.

Beer.

Water.

Coke.

Mayonnaise.

Odds and ends of leftover food that he'd probably bought at the deli.

And very little else.

I smiled as I shut the door, thinking it was a typical bachelor fridge.

I closed my eyes for a moment and just listened to Devon play, letting the music sink into my soul.

He was an extraordinary piano player, and jazz music was hard to play at this level.

Anna hadn't been exaggerating.

Devon was *that* good, not only with his technical skills, but putting emotion into the piece.

I couldn't resist just standing there for a minute, soaking in the joy of listening to an incredible musician.

I finally opened my eyes, knowing that I had to make my presence known. It felt rude to be in his house and not announce myself.

All I had to do was follow the music until I was at the door of his music room.

"I'm here," I announced loudly, hating the fact that the beautiful song stopped the moment that he saw me.

"Sorry," he muttered as he stood up from the grand piano that had been placed in the middle of the room. "I didn't hear you."

God, he looked good.

He was dressed casually in jeans and a white T-shirt with a classic rock band logo on the front.

The shirt looked like he'd had it for a while, and it molded lovingly over his muscular chest and biceps.

Devon might be a jerk sometimes, but I had to admit that he was a gorgeous grump.

"Your playing is phenomenal," I said honestly. "And this room is incredible."

He had top-of-the-line instruments around the massive room along with some that I knew were vintage or antiques.

"Do you play?" he asked curiously as he walked toward me.

"Yes," I admitted. "But not like that. I studied piano from the time I was in grade school, but my skill level is mediocre. I haven't practiced in a long time. Why aren't you a professional musician?"

He grinned as he stopped in front of me. "I had a band when I was in high school. I thought I wanted to be a rock star, but I couldn't sing worth a damn. I can hold a tune, but I didn't have a great voice for a lead singer. That's when I decided it was going to be a hobby. It's a passion of mine, but I'm better at writing music and playing instruments than I am at singing."

"Still," I objected. "You could have been a professional musician without being a singer."

I had my doubts that Devon couldn't sing. Most likely he just preferred not to do it.

He shrugged. "Sometimes you don't always want your passion to be a way to make a living. It can take the fun out of it. I'm happy with the way things turned out. I'm good at what I do, and I manage to work with some creative businesses. You love to cook, and you're incredibly talented at it, but you didn't become a chef for a living."

Devon just kept surprising me.

He thought a lot deeper than the shallow, billionaire playboy I'd always imagined he was.

"You're right," I confessed. "Having to do it every day for long hours probably would take the fun out of a passion. Speaking of food, I made you something that I left in the fridge. And I brought some things to make lunch. I wanted to do something to thank you for teaching me to ride."

He looked surprised. "You didn't have to do that."

"I wanted to," I insisted. "It's not much. It's just lunch and a hummingbird cake."

His grin widened. "I have to admit that I have no idea what's in a hummingbird cake."

I smiled back at him. "It's a southern recipe. Your mom mentioned that you love pineapple. It has pineapple, bananas, a sweet glaze, and pecans."

He raised a brow teasingly. "Sugar? I thought you were preaching at me to eat healthier."

I laughed. "I'm not a health food nut. It's homemade. Natural ingredients. No chemicals. But it does have plenty of sugar. Nobody can be good all the time, and I like to bake. It's not going to top your mom's huckleberry pie or the cinnamon rolls at The Mug And Jug, but it's really good."

"Let's get some coffee and cake," he called out as he exited the music room and headed toward the kitchen. "We can go over safety rules while we're eating."

"It's not typically a breakfast food," I told him as I followed him to the kitchen.

"I'm not a typical guy," he answered mischievously. "Anything with that much good stuff works at any time for me. What did you have for breakfast?"

"Yogurt, fruit, and granola," I shared. "It's my normal breakfast."

"I put something in the microwave," Devon said as I took the cake out of the fridge. "It wasn't enough food. The containers are small."

"Are you trying to justify eating cake for breakfast?" I joked.

"Nope," he replied as he made us both a cup of coffee with his fancy coffee maker. "I very rarely have to justify anything. I was just letting you know why I'm still a little hungry."

That was probably true. He was a billionaire, and he was probably never questioned about anything he did.

His tone was so playful that I didn't take offense. Really, this side of Devon was incredibly…appealing.

I took the piece of cake I'd cut for him, found a plate for it, and put it on the breakfast bar.

He brought forks and the coffees.

"I hope you don't take creamer because I don't have any kind of milk in the house," he said sheepishly as he sat down.

"I usually do," I admitted. "But I can drink it black."

"You're not having any cake?" Devon said unhappily as he sat down.

I unzipped my lightweight jacket and hung it on the back of the chair before I sat down. "I'm good. It's your cake, and I had my breakfast. I gained a few pounds over the winter because I wasn't exercising much, and I was cooking a lot. I'm used to being a little more active."

"You look fine. You don't look like you're carrying any extra pounds." Devon took a large bite of the cake and was silent for a moment while he chewed and swallowed. "Don't tell Mom, but that's better than her huckleberry pie and the cinnamon rolls. It's one of the best things I've ever tasted."

I swallowed a sip of my coffee. "It's one of my favorites, but I don't make it often. I'd eat the whole cake within a few days."

"A few days?" he asked. "This one will probably be gone by tonight."

I snorted. "You can't possibly eat an entire cake in one day."

"Watch me," he warned. "It's not *that* big of a cake, and it's so damn good that it will be calling my name all day and evening. I have a pretty healthy appetite, which is why I have a gym and an indoor pool. I don't think anyone has ever made anything for me before except my mother. It's really appreciated, Reese."

Well, that was kind of…sad.

Everyone needed to be appreciated, even a billionaire who had more money than God.

I supposed that no one thought about making him anything because he could buy anything he wanted.

"What's for lunch?" he asked as he stopped gorging on cake to pick up his coffee mug.

"Chicken burrito bowls. I'll make yours an extra-large one," I teased. "I hope you like Mexican food."

"Love it," he said like he was looking forward to the meal. "Did you bring your swimsuit."

"It's in the car," I replied. "I was juggling the cake and the stuff for the burrito bowls. I'm going to love the exercise."

"I told you that you could come here whenever you want to use the gym," he grumbled.

"I know," I said softly. "And I appreciate the offer, but you're already doing so much for me by teaching me to ride. I'd never want to take advantage of your generosity."

"I'm not really known for being a generous guy," he said drily. "It's not a big sacrifice for me. I ride almost every day, and the gym and pool are downstairs. It doesn't bother me when someone is there. But I'm willing to barter if it will make you feel better."

I raised a brow. "What exactly are we negotiating?"

"If you use the gym after work, I propose that you make dinner and feed me after you're done. Just tell me what supplies you need me to stock, and I'll do it."

I let out a startled laugh. "You're supposed to be a savvy businessman. I have to eat, and I'm going to cook anyway. That's the best you can do?"

He shrugged. "A guy has his personal priorities. I like to eat. I hate to cook, and I can only do really basic stuff. I'd feel like I was making out like a bandit if you make that deal."

I didn't think he was getting much for being inconvenienced, but he looked so hopeful that I said, "Done! Is three times a week okay with you? It would help me take off the pounds I gained over the winter. Once it's a little warmer, I can start walking and hiking."

"Every day would be fine with me," he answered eagerly. "But I'll take what I can get."

I let out a silent sigh.

I wasn't sure what had happened to the disagreeable, unpleasant man that I'd been dealing with for the last several months.

This man was a guy I was starting to like.

Wherever the old Devon had gone, I was hoping I'd seen the last of him.

It probably wasn't a great idea to be spending more time with Devon, but I was starting to discover that this new Devon was pretty irresistible.

Chapter 8

Devon

"You're doing great," I encouraged Reese thirty minutes into our ride.

I was riding behind her on my quarter horse, Thunder, watching her technique and correcting her when necessary.

We'd gone over the basic safety rules as I'd finished the rest of my cake and coffee, and we'd spent some time going over horse behavior and how to tack up Luna before I'd put Reese in the saddle.

I had to give her credit, she'd hefted her own saddle onto Luna easily, and she'd soaked in information like a sponge.

It had been love at first sight for Reese and Luna. Probably the piece of banana I'd given Reese to give her horse had helped Luna warm up to her almost immediately. Luna was picky about her treats, and bananas were her favorite.

The two just seemed to fit each other perfectly, and Reese truly did seem to adore the beautiful Gypsy Vanner. She'd seemed almost enraptured by the horse's flowing mane and tail, and her powerful hindquarters. Reese was the perfect size to ride Luna, and she'd probably been less intimidated by Luna because she wasn't a huge horse.

Reese had just practiced putting Luna into a trot with leg pressure like I'd taught her in the corral before we'd left the stables.

We wouldn't be running any races today, but she was slowly getting the hang of controlling her horse with leg pressure and her reins.

She'd probably get into more advanced stuff faster than I'd thought.

Reese was eager to learn and to ride, and she caught on quickly for a woman who had never ridden.

She wasn't bouncing around in the saddle like most beginners. She had a natural instinct to move with the horse's motion that most beginners didn't pick up right away, and her relaxed posture was balanced after just a few corrections from me.

Still, I'd slapped a helmet on her head in case she took a tumble, but it didn't look like that was going to happen.

Reese's enthusiasm amused me, and I wasn't a guy who was amused by much of anything.

She looked…happy.

She'd been so grateful to get onto a horse that she'd made me a cake…from scratch.

And that made me feel like even more of an asshole.

Hell, I'd appreciated her gesture more than she'd ever know, but I *wasn't* a nice guy.

I wasn't teaching her to ride because I was a good man.

I'd brought her here to pry information out of her.

Having her do something like that for me had caught me off-guard.

I was starting to realize that doing thoughtful things was just part of Reese's nature, and that she was just inherently…kind.

I'd felt so damn guilty that I hadn't asked her a single question that I knew she didn't want to answer.

I couldn't.

For some damn reason I just didn't really want to see fear in her eyes. I'd rather watch her smile and her joy because she was on a horse. We could get to the difficult stuff…later.

I was starting to get addicted to her smile and maybe her happiness was contagious because I was feeling pretty damn happy myself at the moment.

That was pretty unusual for me because I wasn't a guy who experienced a lot of emotional extremes of any kind.

Generally, I was just a cynical bastard who didn't smile very often.

The trail widened so I pulled up beside her. "Having fun?" I asked her.

Her smile was almost blinding, and her cheeks were flushed as she replied, "The most fun I've had in a long time. Thank you so much for this. Luna is a dream horse, and it's almost surreal that I'm actually riding her."

Christ! She was beautiful.

And I was so fucked.

I'd been extremely unsuccessful at convincing my dick that she was the enemy.

Probably because I really didn't believe that myself anymore.

However, she was hiding something, and I was determined to figure out exactly what she didn't want to reveal.

I had to be honest with myself and admit that I hadn't negotiated my gym for dinner with nefarious intentions.

Truth was, I just wanted to see more of Reese. During that time together maybe she'd learn to trust me and tell me what I wanted to know.

I also happened to love everything she cooked.

Win. Win.

At least it was for me.

She seemed to think she was getting a good deal, so neither one of us was unhappy with that agreement.

"You two look good together," I commented. "I think you're a good match."

"I think we're a perfect match," Reese agreed. "You said she came from a top breeder and that she's from a champion lineage. Was she terribly expensive?"

Luna was a special horse, and she hadn't come cheap, but I wasn't about to tell Reese how much my brothers and I had paid for her when we'd gifted her to my mother several years ago.

I suspected that Reese was pondering the idea of asking to buy her from me in the future when she was settled enough to own a horse.

"A good Gypsy Vanner is a little pricey," I said vaguely. "They aren't a common breed in the United States and it's not easy to find a good purebred like her. But I've paid more for a horse."

That actually was the truth. I liked champion bred horses, and I had a lot of them in my barn.

"You're evading the question," she shot back. "I guess that means you aren't going to tell me what she's worth."

"Nope," I agreed as I shot her a grin. "I never reveal the results of a private negotiation."

"Well, she's a beautiful horse. It's sad that your mother can't ride as much as she used to ride."

"It's a limitation she accepted not long ago," I told Reese. "But she's taken up a lot of other hobbies to make up for it. She's become a very avid gardener now, and she keeps busy all the time. I think she was ready to retire from painting, so that didn't bother her much, either."

"I adore your mother. If she ever needs help with anything, please call me. Once I'm proficient at riding, I'd be happy to ride her horse for her when she needs someone to do it."

"The feeling is mutual," I informed her. "Mom talks about you all the time. She said you stop by her place fairly often to check up on her and chat. I appreciate that. She loves company."

She laughed. "I do it for my sake, too. She's had a fascinating life. I've learned a lot from her. She's an amazing cook, and I like the company, too. She's so excited about her first grandbaby."

It occurred to me that Reese could be homesick and possibly a little lonely. She had no one here except Hannah, Lauren, and Anna, and all of them had pretty busy lives.

"Are your parents still alive?" I asked curiously. "Siblings?"

Her happiness dimmed for just a moment and a flash of sadness crossed her expression as she nodded. "I miss them. We've always been close because I was an only child."

"Can't they come and visit?" I questioned.

There it was. That flash of fear in her eyes that I hated, and I almost regretted asking the question.

Was she currently estranged from her parents?

"They're pretty busy right now," she said vaguely. "But I'm hoping that can happen soon. We've always lived in the same city. It seems weird not to see them fairly often. They were a huge part of my life. They've always been my biggest supporters."

"Did they support you coming to Montana?"

She hesitated for a moment before she answered. "Yes. They thought the change would be good for me."

Okay, I *had* to ask the question. "Reese, is one of your old boyfriends harassing you? Is that why you needed a change?"

Her eyes widened. "Is that why you think I moved here? No, that wasn't a factor at all. I haven't had a serious relationship in a long time."

I had to believe her. She'd looked so astonished at the very idea of a problem ex-boyfriend that I didn't think she was lying.

"Have you ever gotten close to getting married?" I asked.

Hell, did I really need to know *that*?

I couldn't figure out why I'd just asked that question, but for some damn reason I really wanted to know.

She shook her head. "Not really. I've never been engaged. Just a few long-term boyfriends."

She was young, so that made sense.

"What happened with them?" I queried wanting to kick myself for asking another question that I didn't need to know.

"They eventually dumped me," she said matter-of-factly. "I don't lead an exciting life, and I was boring. I was in school, and then I worked a lot. I loved to cook, and I do a lot of boring things like antique hunting and crocheting. I always pick the wrong guys. They liked to party, and I was an adult and past my college party days. I was over it, but they weren't. I was willing to go to a club sometimes, but not every single night. So now you know why the idea of some guy being obsessed with me is laughable to me. I never broke up with any of the guys I dated. They dumped *me*."

I wasn't sure why, but the idea of anyone dumping Reese infuriated me.

What in the hell had they been thinking?

Reese was everything a guy could want in a partner,

"You're smart, and they were idiots," I grumbled.

"Thanks for the vote of confidence," she replied. "But I was always kind of a nerd, even in high school. I was in band playing the flute instead of being a cheerleader in the popular crowd. I did a lot of volunteer work with my parents, which isn't exactly exciting. But I'm okay with who I am. I probably wished I fit in better in high school, but as a grown up, I was good with being a little boring because I liked my life. I like helping people when I can. I found good friends that accepted me and had common interests."

"You're perfect the way you are," I told her. "I wasn't part of the popular crowd in high school, either. I played some sports, but I was more into music. There's nothing wrong with being who you are, Reese. I guess you already have that figured out. For what it's worth, I think you're exciting and unique."

I wasn't lying.

For some reason, Reese fascinated the hell out of me.

I wasn't used to women wanting nothing from me and doing nice things for me.

They certainly wouldn't think I was doing them a huge favor by letting them use my gym or teaching them to ride a horse.

"I'm definitely going to take that as a compliment," she said lightly. "Especially since that comment is coming from a gorgeous, extremely accomplished billionaire. Maybe there's still hope that I'll find a decent guy who thinks the same thing someday."

There were plenty of men who'd like to find a beautiful, intelligent, caring woman like Reese. She'd just been unlucky enough to end up with the dimwits.

For some damn reason I didn't really care for the thought of Reese finding that guy.

It was a stupid thing to think since I was starting to like her, but there was a part of me that rejected the idea of seeing her with a love interest.

I shook off that feeling.

I probably just felt that way because I was attracted to her physically.

"We should head back toward the barn," I said abruptly. "It will take us a while to get back, and I think you've had enough for one day."

She tried to hide her disappointment, but I saw it, and I fucking hated it.

"You'll thank me later when you're not limping around from being in a saddle for too long," I added in a more playful tone. "We can take a short ride whenever you're here to use the gym. We'll have a little daylight on some days after work now that spring is here. On Saturdays, we can explore the area on horseback so you're familiar with some of the trails."

"When do you think I'll be ready to ride alone?" she asked.

Fuck! I really didn't like that thought.

"Not for a while," I said noncommittally. "I need to make sure you know exactly what to do if something weird happens. Luna is pretty solid, steady, and well-trained, but anything can happen out here. You're stuck with me until you're comfortable with anything that could pop up."

"I'm happy to have company and someone to teach me," she said thoughtfully. "I just don't want to take up all of your free time."

Hell, that was part of my plan, right? I wanted to spend time with her to get her to trust me.

"Not a problem," I said. "If I get home early enough, I try to get a short ride in anyway, and I'll actually get a decent dinner if you're here."

She let out a genuine laugh, and the sound made my gut ache.

Christ! I really needed to get my attraction to her under control.

I was on a mission to get the truth out of her, and that was my only objective.

The problem was that I wasn't sure that was the *only* reason I'd agreed to spend more time with her anymore.

I hadn't planned on actually enjoying the time I spent with her, and I was going to have to keep reminding myself that once I was satisfied with the information she gave me, that time spent with her would end abruptly.

I fucking ignored my gut and my dick this time when they both rebelled.

I was going to get this shit under control and listen to my reasonable brain from now on.

Chapter 9

Reese

The two weeks that followed my first riding lesson were some
of the happiest days I'd spent in Crystal Fork.

Spring was an unpredictable time in Montana, and we had
some nice days mixed in with some cooler weather.

I'd fallen completely in love with Luna and riding, and I felt better
now that I was getting regular exercise.

Devon's gym had everything a commercial gym had to offer, so
I used his treadmill, and he'd showed me how to do some strength
training.

When he got home early enough to ride, he usually joined me in
the gym and the pool afterward, and then we had dinner together.

The only problem with this whole arrangement was that, at some
point, I'd started to really look forward to spending time with Devon.

At this point, I could actually say that he was…a friend.

Unfortunately, that was a little bit complicated for me because I
was starting to become more and more attracted to my new friend.

How could I not be?

Not only was Devon ridiculously handsome, but he was crazy smart, charming, and we had a lot in common even though we'd lived completely different lives.

For some reason, the two of us had just...clicked.

Maybe because we were both a little quirky and different, so we understood one another perfectly.

There were times when I had to stop myself from reaching out to touch him like my instincts prompted me to do.

Devon Remington could never be anything more than a friend to me, and I had to check my attraction to him.

Honestly, he was getting to know me. I was honest with him as much as I could be, but could we really be friends without him knowing everything about me?

"I heard that you're helping Mom get ready for the spring fundraiser," Devon commented as he inhaled the soup and sandwiches I'd made for lunch today.

It was Saturday, and we'd ridden for hours today. We'd taken a break at the river on Kaleb's property, which was one of my favorite spots on the trails.

The trail system was vast, but I was getting to know my way around the area.

I was completely comfortable on Luna now, and we'd gotten to the point where we could let the horses run to get some real exercise.

My sweet girl would never be able to keep pace with the much larger Thunder, but she was smooth, fast, and powerful.

I'd taken my first fall off Luna's back during my training, and it hadn't been pleasant, but it wasn't Luna's fault.

One moment of distraction while I was watching Devon's ripped body on his horse was all it had taken for me to lose my balance and take a tumble.

I'd gotten my ass up and back on Luna as soon as Devon had decided I wasn't injured.

I'd felt like an idiot, and I certainly hadn't told Devon exactly why I'd lost my balance.

Lesson learned.

No matter how comfortable I was on Luna, getting distracted could get me hurt.

I couldn't ogle the gorgeous man while I was on a horse.

That had happened a week ago and I hadn't fallen since.

I nodded as I swallowed some of my soup at the breakfast bar. "I'll be at her place again tomorrow to help her. It's actually been a lot of fun."

He shook his head. "It's a pain in the ass, but the whole town looks forward to a good outdoor party after a long winter."

Millie had explained to me that although the fundraiser did raise funds for the town, it was actually an annual event that brought the whole town together to gossip, eat, and catch up with each other.

It was more like an annual festival than a true fundraiser, and it was something the town loved to participate in every year.

There would be tons of booths to buy things, food booths, and an auction.

It sounded like fun to me.

"You'll be helping, too," I reminded him.

Devon, Kaleb, and Tanner would be doing a lot of the heavy lifting right before and during the event.

"We always do," he told me. "Most of the guys in town are the unpaid laborers that lug stuff around."

He didn't sound unhappy with his role in the spring fundraiser, and I knew he really didn't mind even though he liked to joke about it being a pain in the ass.

"I've got my eye on that beautiful silver and turquoise necklace the silversmith donated for the auction," I shared with him. "It's such intricate work, but I'm sure it's going to be a popular item. It might be a little out of reach for me."

I was living on the money I made from Glam Anywhere, and although my expenses were low, I wasn't sure I had enough saved to buy the necklace.

Devon eyed me silently for a moment before he responded, "You'll get it. Pete has been selling his stuff here and in Billings for decades. Most people around here already have a piece of his work. It will be popular, but I don't think it will go sky high. Mom's painting will probably be the most popular item. People come from all areas to bid sometimes."

I snorted. "That one is definitely out of reach for me even though I'd love to own it. The price on her art is going up significantly every year."

"It has been since she stopped painting," Devon mused. "There's a limited supply of her work on the market now."

M. Remington paintings had always been pricey, but he was right. When the production stopped, an artist's paintings were even more in demand.

I sighed. "You're lucky to have a number of them hanging in this house."

My heart tripped when he grinned at me mischievously. "And I didn't have to pay for a single one of them. There are perks to being a popular artist's son."

"You're horrible," I said in a teasing voice.

He shrugged. "I never claimed to be nice. I'm a businessman."

"I call bullshit," I said adamantly. "Underneath that suave, professional exterior, you are a nice guy."

He winked at me. "Don't tell anyone. I'm known to be a badass in business."

I'd never seen Devon in action when it came to Remington, but to get where he was today, he probably was a hard negotiator.

I crossed my heart as I promised, "The truth is safe with me."

"Just like anything you ever want to tell me is safe with me," he said in a more somber tone.

My belly tightened at his words. Devon had been hinting at the fact that he knew I was holding something back from him.

I wasn't sure how he knew that because nobody else suspected it.

God, I wanted to spill everything to him so badly, but that just wasn't possible.

I wanted to be honest with all of my friends here, and it killed me that I couldn't completely be myself with them.

"I've told you some of my secrets," I protested, forcing my tone to be upbeat.

He was silent as he scrutinized my face and then looked me directly in the eyes.

Dammit! He was silently asking for something that I just couldn't give him right now.

That moment became so uncomfortable that I broke our eye contact.

"Not all of them," he rumbled.

I wanted to ask him how he knew that, but then I'd be admitting that I wasn't being entirely truthful.

It was an almost unbearable position to be in, and I had to stop myself from squirming in my chair.

It hurt that he couldn't trust me the way I was coming to trust him, but he was incredibly intuitive, and I wasn't about to compound the lies by saying I wasn't hiding anything.

I wasn't a good liar, and there had been enough falsehoods for me since I'd moved to Crystal Fork.

I hated dishonesty, so it was ironic that I'd been forced into this situation.

"Do you trust me, Reese?" Devon asked in a low baritone voice that was as intense as I'd ever heard it.

I nodded. "Yes."

"Then why can't you tell me what's bothering you?"

My heart melted and I gave up trying to pretend that I was holding nothing back.

Somehow, Devon knew that I was withholding some information.

He wasn't guessing or wondering.

He *knew*.

The two of us had some kind of weird chemistry between us, and we were starting to be able to read each other's emotions.

I could sense it.

"There's just some things I can't talk about right now," I confessed, stumbling a little over the words. "It's not dangerous to anyone. It's personal."

He shook his head. "I think I've gotten to know you well enough to realize you'd never intentionally hurt anyone. But something is eating you alive, and if you want to talk about it, I'm here to listen."

"Not now," I said in a voice that was barely a whisper.

He could read me far too well, and I found that a little bit scary.

The whole situation *was* eating me alive, but there was nothing I could do about it.

"Look at me, Reese," he insisted in a guttural voice.

His tone was so insistent that I locked eyes with him almost immediately.

"I can see the turmoil in those beautiful eyes of yours," he rasped as he held my gaze. "Some fear. Some panic. And I fucking hate it. I can wait until you trust me completely. I don't want you to ever feel that way when you're with me."

Tears started to swim in my eyes, and a single tear plopped onto my cheek.

Before I could protest, Devon rose from his chair, picked me up, and sat back down with my body sprawled over his lap.

He wrapped his powerful arms around me, and my whole world felt like it tilted. I wrapped my arms around his neck and started to uncontrollably sob on his shoulder.

I'd held so many emotions back for so long that it was a purging that burst from my heart and soul in an enormous flood of sobs that racked my body to its core.

Devon held me tightly as he soothed, "You're safe with me, Reese. I promise you that."

I believed him.

I felt safe.

I felt like I could be vulnerable with him without fear.

The way that he held me told me that he cared for me.

"I'm so sorry," I said with a hiccup after my crying binge had subsided.

I felt almost listless as my head plopped onto his shoulder.

"Don't be sorry," he said huskily. "Just let me hold you for a minute."

That was an easy request to grant.

It felt so good to finally be this close and this tight with his hard body that I could stay this way for the entire day.

His masculine scent and warm body were sensually enticing, but I tried to push away all of my carnal thoughts and just relax in his arms.

His grip was protective and reassuring, and that was something I'd needed for a long time.

I wasn't sure how long we stayed that way, locked together, with Devon stroking a soothing hand over my back.

I finally lifted my head to thank him.

Our eyes locked, and he spoke before I could get the words out. "Keep your secrets, Reese," he said hoarsely. "But don't feel like you have to lie to me. If you can't talk about something, just tell me. And let me be there for you when you need me."

I nodded my agreement and swallowed hard.

I wasn't sure which one of us moved first, but Devon suddenly put his hand at the nape of my neck and my lips were on his before I could blink, much less speak.

It was an embrace that was unlike anything I'd ever experienced before, and I was swept away by a need and a desire that almost knocked me off his lap.

It was demanding and greedy.

Sensual and hungry.

And bordering on desperation.

He explored my mouth like he owned it, and I opened to his commanding tongue like it was something I'd needed forever.

Heat flooded between my thighs, and I wanted to straddle this man and give him anything he wanted.

I moaned against his lips and threaded my hands into his hair, savoring the feel of those thick locks between my fingers.

God, I wanted this man and all of the pleasure I knew he could give me.

Desperately.

Devon was the one who finally broke contact, his chest heaving. "Fuck! I shouldn't have done that."

My brain was scrambled as I panted. "You're right. We can't do this."

Kissing him like that had been crazy, but I was having an extremely tough time convincing myself that something that had felt so damn good was so damn wrong.

Chapter 10

Devon

"Don't," I ground out as Reese tried to scramble off my lap. I tightened my hold on her and willed my body to relax.

"We need to talk about this," I demanded. "I think it's obvious that I'm attracted to you."

It had to be obvious since the evidence of that attraction was pressing hard against her gorgeous ass.

I was relieved when her body started to relax against me.

I hated myself for bringing those tempting lips against mine, but a stampede of wild horses wasn't going to stop me from kissing her.

However, my brain was now going to check myself.

"I'm definitely not going to claim that I didn't want that," she told me emphatically. "But I shouldn't have kissed you."

I chuckled. I couldn't help it. "I think I was the one who kissed you, sweetheart."

"Whatever," she said in a flippant voice. "I certainly wasn't resisting. I was participating enthusiastically. I guess it's apparent that I'm attracted to you, too."

Damn! I loved to hear those words from her lips, even though I shouldn't be ridiculously glad that she'd said them out loud.

This attraction between us couldn't go anywhere, but I wanted her to want me.

That was probably a little twisted, but I didn't give a shit.

"I can never be the man you need and deserve, Reese," I said honestly.

"And you really don't know everything about me," she rationalized. "I know it was wrong, but I don't regret it. I can't. But I know things can't go any further between the two of us."

I couldn't honestly say I regretted it, either.

But that taste of Reese had just made me want her more.

Fuck! I really was screwed.

My feelings for Reese had morphed into something different over the last two weeks.

Yeah, I still wanted her in my bed moaning my name while she had multiple orgasms.

But I felt weirdly protective of her, too.

I wasn't trying to pry information out of her anymore. I'd given up when my protective instincts had taken over.

I cared about her.

I didn't want her to be afraid anymore.

And I wasn't worried that she'd ever hurt anyone in my family.

Did I want her to tell me her secrets?

Hell, yes, I did, but not at the price of her sanity.

I wanted her to feel safe enough that she could tell me anything before that happened.

I needed her to trust me, and I was an impatient asshole.

Real trust was going to take some time.

"So no more kissing," Reese said firmly. "I consider you my friend, Devon."

Hell, I would have been honored to hear that if I didn't want to fuck her six ways to Sunday.

There was definitely a friendship dynamic in this relationship, but that sure as hell wasn't *all* there was to our relationship.

"What happens if we slip up and do it again in the future?" I asked in a frustrated tone.

I couldn't guarantee that it wouldn't happen again, although I'd try to avoid it.

If Reese was anywhere near me, I wanted her.

All I could promise her was that I'd try not to let it happen again.

She let out an adorable little snort against my shoulder. "Then I guess we'll tell each other it can't happen again one more time." She lifted her head to look at me. "I'd do the friends with benefits thing with you in a heartbeat if I didn't feel like it was wrong because I can't tell you everything. I've never done that before, but I'd do it with you."

My dick twitched, and it was screaming at me to try to get her into that type of arrangement. However…

I shook my head. "You need to find the right guy for you. You deserve to find someone who can give you everything you need, not just multiple orgasms."

It almost killed me to say that, but I knew it was true.

Her eyes widened in mock surprise. "Multiple? That's a little bit cocky. Especially since I'm not the kind of woman who does multiple orgasms."

It felt strangely normal to discuss sex with Reese, which was odd.

I didn't usually talk about sex with a woman.

We just…did it.

I shrugged. "I guarantee you can be."

Her cheeks started to flush, which was the cutest thing I'd ever seen.

I hadn't known any women who blushed about anything sexual.

"It's never happened," she said in a slightly flustered voice. "Generally, it doesn't even happen a first time."

"That's only because you've never been with the right guy," I informed her bluntly. "A real man makes sure his woman is satisfied."

I didn't stop her this time when she slipped off my lap.

She fanned herself with her hand. "I think I need a little space."

I smirked. "Getting a little warm? We're human, Reese. Humans like good, hot, sweaty sex."

"I'm starting to think I've never really had good sex," she muttered as she plopped back into her chair. "Let's change the subject, please."

"You started it with the friends with benefits thing," I protested.

"I know," she said with a sigh. "But that was probably a mistake. I think you might be a little too hot for me to handle."

"I think that's exactly what you want," I mused. "I think you've just never asked for what you deserve."

What kind of idiots had she been with in the past?

None of those bastards had deserved a responsive, passionate woman like Reese, that was for sure.

"It's hard to ask for what you want when the guy is drunk and just back from a party," she shot back.

"You deserve a lot more than that," I said gruffly.

"I know," she said woefully. "That's why I haven't had a boyfriend in a long time. I wasn't making good choices. I decided I was better off alone until I could find someone who really cared about me."

"And there were no prospects?" I questioned.

"I guess it really hasn't been my priority," she confessed. "And it's not easy to meet a nice guy, even in a bigger city. I'm not much of a clubber anymore, and I haven't tried dating apps. I did a few blind dates with friends of friends, but they were a disaster. We just didn't...click. And I absolutely won't date somebody from the same workplace. I think that's trouble waiting to happen. Who wants to keep running into an ex-boyfriend at work if it doesn't work out?"

I had to agree with her. I never hooked up with anyone I worked with at the office. That would be awkward, especially since I was the boss.

"I think I finally got philosophical about the whole dating thing," she informed me. "I guess it will happen when it happens."

"Everyone in town will start to try to fix you up with their single relatives pretty soon," I warned her.

She laughed. "It's already happening. I've been working with some of your mother's friends on the spring fundraiser. All of them are throwing me prospects."

Oh, hell no!

For some reason I didn't really want to see Reese dating someone in town.

"And?" I prompted.

"Um…it was a no to all of them," she confided. "I don't want to date anyone right now, Devon. It's not the right time for me."

I hated myself for being relieved, but I was.

"I don't think you're missing anything," I said. "The townspeople aren't particularly good matchmakers. They just want to see everyone married and happy. Especially their single relatives. There aren't a lot of single people here. A lot of my friends got married to their high school sweethearts and stayed to raise their families here. It's rare that someone like you moves here voluntarily."

"I have to admit that I actually like it here," she shared. "It's different. The pace is slower. But it's a beautiful place with friendly people who all help each other. It's a real…community."

"Sometimes that's a pain in the ass, but I missed it when I lived in New York," I told her honestly. "I had my brothers there, but I missed the wide-open spaces and being able to see the stars at night. I craved the sounds of nature and the peace of silence that you can never get in a big city. I missed that sense of a tightknit community when I didn't have it anymore. I grew up on a ranch, and it's probably in my blood. I ride as often as possible to make up for the years that I couldn't."

"You're so good with your horses," she said. "I'm sure you learned all of that from your parents."

"Mostly my dad," I admitted.

"I'm sure you miss him," she said gently.

"Every single day," I answered. "It was a tough time in all of our lives when he died, but we got through it together. It was a wake-up call for all of us not to take anything for granted. Life is short, which is why we all try to find our personal lives outside of work now. Remington was our life for a while. We grew up enough to realize that work isn't our entire lives."

"I admire that about you," Reese said. "You're a billionaire. It would be really easy to get caught up in the power and that lifestyle and make it your entire life. You don't."

"Oh, I did," I answered. "All three of us did. That's why Tanner and Hannah broke up years ago. We all had our heads up our asses and weren't paying attention to our real priorities. Luckily, the knucklehead got a second chance. That's definitely not happening again."

Reese got up and started to grab the dishes. "Hannah told me a little about what happened. The two of them are really happy now, but that separation was hard for both of them."

I took the dishes from her hands. "Hey, cleanup is my job. You cook; I take care of the dishes."

She picked up my dishes and followed me to the sink. "I can help. I'm not going anywhere. I'm just trying to let my food settle before I work out since you insisted on eating first."

I'd been starving by the time we'd finished our long ride, so I'd talked her into getting food first today.

"I was hungry," I grumbled.

Reese actually giggled. "You're always hungry."

"What about that banana bread you brought today?" I asked hopefully.

She sent me a scolding look. "Later. You said you wanted to work out with me, and you can't have a bunch of food on your stomach right before you work out."

I knew better, but I'd done it a number of times anyway.

Since I wasn't really hungry anymore, I let Reese have her way.

We made short work of cleanup, and that's when I noticed that things had changed a little between the two of us.

I invaded her personal space, and she had no problem invading mine.

I'd never realized how much we'd had to work *not* to touch each other before that kiss when we were in close quarters.

That short interlude had changed everything between the two of us, and that probably wasn't a good thing.

Before that kiss, I'd avoided touching her physically.

Since that kiss, all I fucking wanted to do was touch her.

From now on, I was going to have to listen to my head and not my body or my instincts.

I'd had some hard challenges in my life, but something told me that not touching Reese again was going to be one of the hardest things I'd ever had to do.

Chapter 11

Reese

"I 'll have the usual, Silas," I told the older man as I sat on a barstool at The Mug And Jug. "And a decaf for Hannah, please."

It had just become habit for me to stop at The Mug And Jug at least two days a week for coffee before I went to the office.

Hannah and I were both addicted to Silas's mocha lattes, but hers had to be decaf due to her pregnancy.

Today was Wednesday, and it was one of those days that I really needed a coffee to take to work.

"You alone?" Silas asked as he started making my coffees with a lot more pep than most people his age. "Where's that young man of yours today?"

I sent him a chastising look, but he just grinned back at me.

"You know he's not *my* young man," I said teasingly. "And Devon is in Los Angeles on business this week."

It had been over two weeks since that crazy kiss we'd shared, and I'd thought things would be awkward between us, but it actually didn't turn out that way. We'd gotten even closer as friends, and he met me here in the morning when I was stopping for coffee. I was fairly sure he was almost always here at The Mug And Jug before he went to work anyway.

Unfortunately, I was almost certain that two large cinnamon rolls and a coffee were his usual breakfast items during the work week.

It was almost criminal that he could manage to stay so fit on the diet he ate, but he worked out pretty hard in the evenings. He pushed himself a lot harder than I did. And he was pretty active with community and home tasks that needed to be done when he had the time to spare.

Devon had left Sunday evening in his private jet so he could be ready for an early meeting in Los Angeles on Monday.

One of his brothers usually dropped him off so he didn't have to leave a vehicle at the remote airstrip, but I'd insisted on doing it to help him out.

He'd texted me Sunday evening to let me know he was there safely.

We'd started exchanging text messages during the day just to share something funny or just to say good morning and goodnight.

I wasn't exactly sure how that had started, but it was normal for us now to share things sometimes during the day.

"You miss him?" Silas asked gruffly.

I nodded. "He's become a good friend."

"Do you want my advice?" Silas asked as he put a lid on my coffee and started Hannah's.

I smiled at the older man, knowing he was going to give me that advice, whether I wanted it…or not.

Honestly, I didn't mind. There was a lot of wisdom in most of his words that some people probably didn't notice because Silas tended to give his advice very freely and often.

"I've known Devon since the day that boy was born," Silas explained. "I've never seen him look at a woman the way he looks at you. I think you feel the same way. Go after what you want and don't end up living with regrets. Life is too short for that. I told him the same thing."

Okay, he must have chatted with Devon on one of the days that I wasn't here. "Silas, we're friends. You know Devon doesn't do committed relationships, and I respect that decision."

"Nah," Silas responded. "That's a big bunch of horse manure. That was his choice for years, but the right woman can change everything for a man. It's not like he's not capable of doing it. He's just chosen not to because he's never met the right one. I don't know what happened to that boy, and it really doesn't matter. But he doesn't trust easily. Behind his jokes and his cynicism, he's just a regular guy. He really doesn't want to end up alone. He's just chosen not to trust anyone, so he's convinced himself that he can't or doesn't want to commit."

I winced a little when he'd mentioned the fact that Devon didn't trust easily.

I knew that was true, and I was the last woman that he should trust.

I'd been living a lie since the moment I'd driven into town months ago.

Guilt gnawed at me relentlessly every single day.

The closer I got to people in this town, the guiltier I felt.

The closer I got to Devon the more I'd realized that something probably had happened to bring on the distrusting, cynical side of his personality. It definitely wasn't part of his nature. He'd been raised by the same parents as Tanner and Kaleb. By all accounts, he'd had an incredible childhood.

However, I couldn't expect him to share his secrets when I couldn't share mine.

He had a right to hold back whatever he wanted from me.

And he had absolutely no reason to trust me.

"He trusts you," Silas said like he'd just read my mind.

I lifted a brow. "How do you know that?"

"What man gives a woman he doesn't trust a key to his mansion?" he asked.

My eyes widened even more. "How do you know I have a key to his place?"

Devon *had* given me the key to his home so I could go there after work to use the gym and the pool while he was gone.

He actually locked his doors when he was away.

Silas grinned. "Someone saw you heading out toward his place yesterday after work. Word gets around here pretty quickly."

"Then you already knew he was out of town," I said suspiciously.

He nodded. "I knew. I was just giving you a hard time about Devon because I know that you two are sweet on each other. Everyone knows everything that happens here. People have been talking about you two for weeks now."

"We're not—"

"You are," Silas said, cutting off my protest. "You're both just too hardheaded to realize it yet. And please don't give me the excuse that you're just friends. You're both romantically interested. I just can't figure out why you're not dating. Do you want to fill me in?"

No. No, I really didn't want to explain that. "It's complicated, Silas," I muttered.

"Life is complicated, Reese," he said wryly. "Look, I know you didn't come here because you were longing to live in Crystal Fork, Montana. My guess is you're running away from something. But whatever that is, don't let it ruin something that could be good for you."

God, I really wished that I could just tell him why Devon and I couldn't be together, even if Devon decided he wanted some kind of relationship, but that wasn't possible.

I knew Silas was trying to help me, and I was grateful that he cared enough to try, but there was no help for my situation right now.

I shot him a small smile. "Thanks for the advice."

What else could I say?

"Just tell me this," Silas requested. "Do you ever plan on telling Devon that you're interested?"

I stopped trying to pretend that Devon was just a friend. Silas obviously knew that there was some kind of chemistry between the two of us. "I care about him" I said honestly. "But I'm not sure what the future holds for me."

Silas snorted. "It will hold happiness if you'd give that boy a nudge. I don't think it would take much. He already talks about you like he thinks everything you do for him is a miracle. And I might be old, but I'm still a man. I can see when another man is attracted to a woman. Take your time but do me a favor and don't hurt him.

Something tells me that boy has already seen a world of hurt in his past."

My heart ached at his words because I knew he was probably right. "I would never intentionally hurt, Devon. He means the world to me."

That much was absolutely true.

In a brief period of time, Devon had wormed his way into my heart, and I had a feeling if anyone was going to end up hurt, it was going to be me.

Yes, I knew that Devon was attracted to me, but I didn't think he was interested in having a real relationship.

Even if he was interested and had changed his mind about dating, I couldn't date anyone at this point in my life.

"Glad to hear that," Silas said with a grin. "Your coffee is ready. Cinnamon roll?"

I looked longingly at the tray of sweets on the bar.

I'd managed to drop two pounds, and that delicious cinnamon roll was full of calories.

"Life is short. Have a cinnamon roll," Silas teased. "You know you want it."

I let out an exasperated sigh. "Okay, give me one. I'll split it with Hannah. She's still craving sweets. She'll love it, too."

Hannah had tried so hard to resist those cravings, so she didn't have a lot of baby weight once her pregnancy was over. Her cravings had been out of control during her second trimester, but the craving for anything and everything was starting to subside now that she was in her third trimester. The only thing she couldn't quite get under control was her craving for sweets.

I knew that she was eating pretty healthy, so half a cinnamon roll wasn't going to hurt her.

I watched as Silas boxed up the treat, put it in a bag and added two forks to the bag.

I started to dig in my purse, but Silas shook his head. "I'll put it on your tab."

I nodded. Although the whole concept of having a tab somewhere was foreign to me, that was the way Silas operated.

Strangely, my tab was never as much as I thought it should be at the end of every month.

He'd always waved me off and said that I got a frequent visitor discount.

My guess was that he was a big softie and gave working women a significant discount.

"You're the best," I said as I took the bag and gave him a peck on the cheek.

I really did adore Silas, even his unrequested advice.

He always meant well, and he genuinely cared about the people in Crystal Fork.

He sent me a mischievous smile. "If that's true, then forget about Devon and go out on a date with me."

I was used to his mock flirtatiousness, so I wasn't surprised by the comment. "You're too much of a player for me, Silas. But I adore you."

"Can't blame a guy for trying," he grumbled as he handed me the coffees.

"Have a good day. Take care of yourself and don't forget that nutrition shake with lunch," I called out as I headed for the door.

The doctor had told Silas that he was lacking the proper nutrition for a man his age, so he'd insisted on supplements.

He'd hated the taste of it, so he'd refused to drink it.

I'd found him one that tasted better than the one the doctors had suggested, and he'd finally started to drink it every day.

"I'll drink it," he promised. "It tastes a lot better than the awful stuff the doctor gave me. It tastes even better with a little ice cream."

I laughed as I headed out the door.

At Silas's age, I wasn't about to scold about adding ice cream to the drink.

He had zero issues with his blood sugar.

He was getting what he needed nutritionally.

If he wanted it with ice cream, he deserved it for getting down a supplement he really didn't want to take.

Hannah wasn't in the office yet when I got there, but I knew it would only be a matter of minutes before she arrived.

My phone pinged with a text right as I was putting the coffee and cinnamon roll on my desk.

I smiled as I read it.

Devon: *Please don't tell me that you got coffee from The Mug And Jug this morning. I'd have to be jealous. I'm going through withdrawals this morning, and I need a damn cinnamon roll.*

Me: *I'm staring at the mocha lattes I got for me and Hannah right now. And the cinnamon roll we're going to split. I know. I suck. But I don't feel guilty. You're in Los Angeles where you can get anything your stomach desires.*

As we bantered back in forth by text, my heart ached just a little because I really did miss Devon. I'd become so used to him being part of my life that it just didn't feel right when we weren't doing things together in the evening. We'd never really stuck to the three times a week thing. We were together almost every weeknight and on Saturday.

Stop it, Reese. He'll be back on Friday.

The spring fundraiser was coming up this Saturday, so he was going to make it a point to get back as early as possible on Friday to help out.

I'd live until I saw his handsome face again.

I tried not to think too far into the future.

After all, I probably wouldn't stay in Crystal Fork forever, and there would come a day when I'd never see his gorgeous face again. *Ever.*

Because that thought hurt so badly, I quickly pushed it out of my head.

I had to live one day at a time right now, and I'd deal with that situation when it happened.

Chapter 12

Devon

I was beyond ready to land at our private airstrip in Crystal Fork. I didn't think I'd ever anticipated coming home this much in my entire life.

Maybe because I knew that Reese was going to meet me at the airstrip to pick me up.

Fuck! I'd missed her beautiful face, and I'd only been away for five damn days.

I'd gotten used to seeing her gorgeous face and her smile every day, and now I was addicted to both of those things.

I'd been a cranky asshole all week. Even in meetings I'd been abrupt and impatient, which wasn't my normal.

I'd never been so happy to wrap up a business deal as I had been last night, and I'd gotten the hell out of Los Angeles as early as possible this morning.

I hadn't even argued when Reese had told me that Hannah had insisted that she take the day off so she could come pick me up and welcome me home.

If Reese didn't have vacation time accumulated yet, I'd happily pay Hannah not to dock her check.

Hell, I *wanted* to see her.

I wanted to catch up and see if I'd missed anything about her life while I'd been gone.

Yeah, we'd texted every day, but I was quickly realizing that texting didn't cut it for me.

I wanted to see her face.

I wanted to hear her voice again, even if she was giving me hell for something.

I unbuckled my seatbelt and was out of my seat the moment the plane came to a stop.

By the time the pilot opened the exit door and lowered the stairs, I was so eager to get out of the plane that I bolted down the steps.

I jogged toward Reese the moment I saw her standing next to her compact SUV.

I stopped abruptly in front of her and just soaked in her welcoming, radiant smile.

"Hi," she said softly as she put a welcoming hand on my arm. "Welcome home. I missed you."

Fuck this shit!

Although I wanted to hear that she'd missed me, I needed more than a polite greeting at the moment.

I dropped my bag, pulled her into my arms, and kissed her like a lover who had been away for months.

The small moan deep in her throat and the fact that she quickly wrapped her arms around my neck was all of the encouragement I needed to kiss her like a man possessed.

I lost my head so badly that I was never quite sure how long we stayed locked in that passionate embrace in the middle of the airstrip, but I didn't give a shit.

I finally had what I'd been wanting all damn week, and I wasn't letting her go before I was ready to do it.

Fuck knew that I wanted a whole lot more, but I'd take whatever I could get from her to try to satisfy the primitive instincts I had for this woman.

She made me crazy, and I was damn tired of trying to pretend that she didn't.

"I missed you, too," I said in a husky voice when we finally came up for air.

"We just did it again," she said breathlessly, not sounding the least bit repentant.

I shook my head. "I don't give a shit," I told her as I stoked her silky, auburn hair. "And I'm not going to say we shouldn't have done it or that it will never happen again. I'm sick of pretending that I can keep the chemistry between the two of us under control. I can't."

"Okay," she agreed happily as she stroked a lock of hair from my forehead. "I'm sick of pretending, too. Feel free to kiss me whenever you want. Touch me whenever you want. Take me up on that friends with benefits offer if you want, and you're sure you can go to bed with a woman you don't know completely. I'm tired of everything, Devon. All I know is that I want you like I've never wanted another man in my entire life. I don't care if you don't give me forever. I'm living my life day by day, and I really don't want to have regrets."

Christ! How was I supposed to respond to *that?*

I wanted Reese in the same way she wanted me, and it was hell knowing that she was willing to have a fling on my terms.

Maybe I didn't know everything about her, but my gut trusted her.

"You deserve more than a fling," I said hoarsely as I ran my finger down the soft skin of her cheek.

"What if I don't want more than that?" she asked as our gazes locked together. "What if I can never have more than that? What if I just want to take whatever I can have right now because there can't be anything else? I'm starting to think that something is better than nothing. You don't want a commitment, and I honestly can't have one right now. Does that really mean we shouldn't grab what happiness and pleasure we can find at the moment?"

I didn't know what in the hell she was saying, but I definitely understood her point.

"Just think about it," she suggested. "I'm not asking you to take me to bed today or tomorrow. I just wanted you to know that I feel different today than I did two weeks ago. I've been cautious all of my life. Maybe having a fling would be good for me, but you're the only guy I'd ever trust enough to take that leap."

Hell, it was ironic that I finally had her trust, but now I didn't want to push her for information she didn't want to give me yet.

Think about it?

I'd probably do nothing else now that she'd told me that she was willing.

Every sexual fantasy I had now revolved around Reese, and a big part of me wanted to act out every one of those fantasies with her.

But the way that I cared about her made everything so damn complicated.

"Let's go home," I said as I took her hand and picked up my bag.

"Are you angry because I spilled all that information?" Reese asked after we'd gotten settled into her vehicle with her at the wheel. "You're pretty quiet right now."

Her SUV was small, so it wasn't comfortable for a large guy like me to drive in the confined space, and it was her vehicle.

"Not at all," I replied as I put the seat back as far as it would go to try to accommodate my long legs. "I always want you to be honest with me about how you feel. I guess I'm just trying to adjust to the fact that you just offered me your body as well as your friendship. I'm glad you trust me."

"I hear a 'but' in there somewhere," she probed.

"There's not," I assured her. "I care about you, Reese, and that makes things a little complicated."

"It really doesn't have to be," she said nonchalantly. "I think our friendship is solid enough to stay friends once the lust part of the relationship burns out for us."

Yeah, but there was a problem with that. I wasn't sure I'd ever get my fill of Reese once I'd been inside her.

I had a feeling I'd always want more.

"And if it doesn't burn out?" I asked.

"I'm sure it will for you," she said stoically. "It doesn't sound like you've stayed hooked up with a woman for long."

I couldn't take offense because her observation was true.

"I can't say that I was friends with any of them, and I never wanted them in the same way I want you," I said a little defensively.

Reese wouldn't be just another hookup for me.

She didn't look at me because she was driving toward my place as she replied reasonably, "Then we see what happens and communicate. When you're ready to end it, we'll stop. I doubt that I'll be the first one to want to stop. Especially if you're capable of making me orgasm."

Her tone was teasing, like she wanted to put a little levity into the serious discussion.

"You just got back from a long business trip," she explained. "I shouldn't have dumped that on you the moment you got off the jet. Let's relax for a while and forget that I even said anything. It's been a long week for you, Devon."

There was no way in hell that I was going to forget that she'd offered me her body.

But maybe she was right about changing the subject.

My cock was so hard that my balls were turning blue.

"Tell me what I missed while I was gone," I suggested.

"Not a whole lot," she shared. "Not a lot changes in Crystal Fork in five days. I think we're ready for the fundraiser tomorrow. We're just going to need help hauling stuff around at the park early in the morning. I visited Luna every day and gave her some love and a piece of banana, but she was sad because we couldn't go out and ride. I promised you that I wouldn't ride without you while you were gone, but I think you need to cut me loose to ride on my own."

"Not yet," I grumbled.

Technically, Reese could probably do some rides on the trails by herself, but the thought of something happening to her as a novice rider on her own still worried me.

She was getting pretty familiar with some of the trails, but anything could happen from an unexpected wildlife encounter to meeting up with someone who didn't belong on our property.

I always carried a firearm out on the trails as a precaution.

"I think I should teach you to shoot so you have some kind of protection while you're out on the trails alone," I added.

She shook her head emphatically. "I don't think I could shoot an animal, even to protect my own life. Couldn't I just carry bear spray. It works on all mammals, right?"

It wasn't as effective as carrying a weapon, but it could work.

"Do you know how to use it?"

She nodded. "I used to carry it when I was hiking. I've never had to use it, but I know how and I'm okay with using it."

"I'll get some and then we'll talk about you riding alone."

I'd probably stall around for a while to give myself a little more time before I cut her loose to ride out on her own, but I was eventually going to have to do it.

"Thank you," she said as she sent me a quick, heart stopping smile.

Seeing Reese happy had become a fucking mission for me, and if she kept smiling at me like that, for the first time in my life, I was going to be willing to give a woman everything she wanted... and more.

Chapter 13

Reese

The spring fundraiser had been a huge success so far. I swore that most of the people in Crystal Fork were here at the fundraiser, and probably some from other areas as well. It was crowded, but it had been such a fun day.

I loved arts and crafts, and I had a bagful of goodies stashed in the booth that Millie was overseeing.

"The auction is going to start soon," I told Devon as we strolled around and looked at the items to be auctioned. "Have you had your fill of the food yet?"

I stroked my forefinger lightly over the beautiful turquoise and silver necklace.

I wasn't going to get my hopes up, but I was hoping Devon was right and that I could put in the winning bid.

There were other incredible things to be auctioned off, including a beautiful painting of Millie's, but the intricate necklace was the only thing I planned on bidding on.

"Never," he said with a grin. "I'll go back for dessert later."

I wasn't sure how he could even think about dessert after all of the food he'd eaten, but he'd worked pretty hard earlier in the day.

As things had wound down a little, Millie had waved us away to go enjoy the things the fundraiser had to offer.

Devon had immediately headed for the food booths, but we'd gotten around to most of the stalls after his hunger was satisfied.

We hadn't really talked much about my offer of friends with benefits that I'd stupidly blurted out the day before.

Today, I still didn't know what I'd been thinking.

Maybe it was the excitement of seeing him come home and that stunning welcome home kiss.

Maybe it was something Silas had said that had gotten me thinking.

Or...maybe I'd just had a change of heart.

I didn't want to have regrets, and I'd never felt as close to a man as I did to Devon.

The chemistry between the two of us was almost palpable in the air around us whenever we were together.

I wanted to know what it would feel like to be with someone who cared about me and would probably make me shatter into a million pieces in bed.

I'd get that from Devon, and it would be a first for me.

I didn't want to pass on the opportunity to feel that way.

I knew if I did, I'd probably regret it in the future.

I wasn't a woman who threw caution to the wind, but if there was ever a man worth doing that for, I was looking at him right now.

Devon leaned down and grumbled beside my ear, "If you don't stop looking at me like that, I'm going to kiss you right here in front of the entire town."

"Like what?" I said with surprise.

He straightened up and lifted a cocky brow. "Like you'd like to have both of us naked right now with my head between your gorgeous legs. You were thinking about sex. Admit it."

God, could he really read my thoughts that easily?

"You have lust on your mind, sweetheart. I can see it in your eyes, and I recognize that look because it's the same way I look at you."

Our gazes locked, and the intensity of his stare sent searing heat between my thighs. I didn't know exactly what he was thinking, but I definitely knew it was carnal.

"You can't kiss me in front of the entire town," I said, tripping over the words.

"I can't?" he said in a low, husky baritone. "Watch me. You did give me permission to touch you whenever I wanted. I want, Reese. I've been wanting since you strolled out of your apartment this morning in those jeans and that skimpy top."

It was warm today, and since I knew I'd be doing physical work, I'd dressed appropriately.

I wouldn't say the crop top I was wearing was skimpy, but my skinny jeans were form-fitting because they were older and had been washed repeatedly. The crop top was just short enough to see a tiny bit of skin when I moved.

Apparently, that was enough for Devon because he was looking at me like he was starving, and I was his entrée.

It was heady to have a man like Devon look at me like this.

I wondered how I'd never noticed the way that he looked at me before this very moment.

Silas had obviously noticed.

I'd probably been too caught up in fighting my own emotions to notice that he was feeling the same way I did.

"I'm going to end up taking you up on that deal. You know that, right?" he asked in a come-fuck-me voice that made me half crazy. "I'd like to be a better man and leave you alone so you can find your dream guy, but I'm actually a selfish asshole."

My heart stuttered as I asked, "Are you? Please don't feel pressured to—"

"Fuck! I don't feel pressured," he interrupted. "I feel like I'm going to lose it if I don't get you into my bed. But this can't be just friends with benefits for us. A hookup isn't going to work for me. Not with you."

I wanted to ask him what he meant, but my words were cut off as I saw the Chief Of Police jogging toward me waving his arms in the air.

"It's Ralph," I told Devon. "Something is wrong."

He turned and watched as the older man approached us.

When he arrived, his expression was grim. "We need you, Reese," he said in a troubled voice.

"What's happening?" I asked.

"Gloria is in trouble. I think she's in labor. Something's not right. She's at Millie's booth. I'm sorry to do this—"

"Don't be,' I insisted as I hauled ass toward Millie's booth with Ralph and Devon right behind me.

There was no doctor in Crystal Fork.

People drove to Billings for their healthcare.

"Gloria is having really bad contractions almost continuously," Ralph told me as we ran. "Her husband said she's had a previous precipitous labor if that means anything to you."

"Shit!" I cursed. "Somebody needs to call an ambulance to get here from Billings as soon as possible."

"I'm on it," Ralph said as he pulled his phone out of his pocket.

I arrived at the booth to see a woman that was obviously in hard labor. She was on a pile of blankets behind that booth so that she was out of sight of onlookers.

Anna and Hannah were kneeling beside Gloria with what had to be her husband on the other side of the pregnant woman.

Millie was standing close by with a worried expression on her face.

"Ambulance is on the way," Ralph yelled from the other side of the booth. "What else can I do?"

I looked up at him from the kneeling position between Gloria's legs that I'd dropped into seconds ago.

I locked eyes with the Chief of Police and said, "I'm going to have to tell her."

He nodded grimly.

"Can you get everyone out of the area right now," I asked him abruptly.

I rattled off several things that I needed, and Ralph took off on a scavenger hunt to see what he could find.

"Gloria," I called softly as I took her hand. "My name is Reese. I'm a women's health nurse practitioner. Before that, I was a labor and delivery nurse. Can I take a look to see how you're progressing?"

The woman looked relieved as she panted and nodded her head between contractions.

"Are you her husband?" I asked the man beside her.

"Yes, I'm Tim. I didn't know this would happen. She's only thirty-seven weeks. We were going to head to Billings to stay with family right after the fundraiser just to be safe. I barely got her to the hospital with our first child. She's been having those false contractions on and off for a while now. The doctor said it was nothing to worry about. She didn't even know she was in labor until her water broke. The contractions started coming hard and fast right after that. I was afraid we wouldn't make it to the hospital before she delivered. I didn't know what to do."

Okay, now I understood why they weren't immediately in a panic when she started having a few contractions. Braxton Hicks contractions weren't that unusual. Gloria obviously hadn't known that she was in labor when her contractions were first starting.

A woman who had experienced precipitous labor with a first child was more likely to have it happen a second time.

A precipitous labor was lightning fast and possibly life-threatening for both the mother and child if they didn't have proper medical intervention.

The couple was smart to take precautions to stay in Billings for the last few weeks of her pregnancy.

Unfortunately, this little peanut obviously had a mind of their own.

"It's not your fault," I said soothingly as I lifted Gloria's sundress to take a look at her progress. "Do you know if you're having a boy or a girl?"

"Girl," he answered, his eyes wide with fear.

I needed to calm this expectant father down.

Since her labor had gone so fast last time, he'd never really had a chance to be a delivery coach.

He was also probably worried because he'd been through a precipitous birth with his wife before.

Luckily, Gloria seemed calmer than he did right now.

I wished I had a bright light right now, but I didn't need a spotlight to see what was happening.

Crap! She's already fully dilated.

At the rate that she was progressing, this baby was going to be born right here in the park before the ambulance arrived.

We certainly couldn't shove her in a car or even one of the Remington helicopters at this point.

This baby was coming *now*.

I'd worked in an office setting with an OB/GYN physician before I'd moved to Crystal Fork. I did a lot of prenatal care, but I'd never delivered a baby by myself. I wasn't a midwife, so I wasn't licensed to deliver a baby on my own. I'd assisted with a ton of high-risk deliveries when I'd been a labor and delivery nurse, but I'd only had one experience with a doctor not arriving before the delivery.

However, since there wasn't a doctor in sight, I was all she had right now.

"Got what I could find," Ralph said as he tossed some items to me and put a bottle of saline and antiseptic on the counter. "I'll go look for more stuff. Kaleb and Tanner are helping me."

All I could think was bless the townspeople in Crystal Fork.

Some of them had obviously had some medical supplies that they'd given up for a fellow citizen in distress.

The rubber gloves weren't sterile, but they were better than nothing.

I quickly doused my hands, the gloves, and my forearms with the antiseptic before I pulled on the gloves.

This wasn't going to be sterile by any means, but I wanted Gloria to be as clean as possible.

"Ralph!" I shouted before he was out of hearing range.

"Yeah!" he called back.

"How far out is that ambulance?"

There was silence for a moment before he answered. "ETA is about fourteen minutes."

I took the pad that he'd brought and scooted it beneath Gloria.

"They aren't going to make it in time, are they?" Hannah asked fearfully.

I glanced at Gloria's progress and shook my head subtly.

"What can I do to help?" she questioned.

Since Hannah was fully versed in the childbirth procedure, I told her, "Stay calm and help keep Gloria calm. She's crowning. You know what that means. Keep her relaxed and tell her not to push right now. Pant with her if you have to. You know the routine."

Hannah nodded and brushed a lock of hair from Gloria's head as she took her hand and helped her pant through her contraction. Anna tried to calm Gloria, too, and added her soothing voice to Hannah's.

Tim tried to assist, but he looked like he was about to fall over himself.

The poor guy looked like he was in a full-blown panic attack.

"Tim?" I said softly.

He turned his wild eyes to mine.

"It's going to be okay. Try to stay calm for Gloria. This will all be over soon. She needs you right now."

He nodded slowly, and his panic seemed to calm a little as he realized he needed to be strong for his wife.

"You're right," he said as he wiped the sweat from his forehead. "I have to keep my shit together."

"You're doing fine," I said soothingly. "It's okay to be nervous, but the ambulance will be here in a few minutes. You'll be seeing your baby girl shortly."

He took a deep breath and let it out. "I'm never going to do this again. Two kids are enough."

I smiled at him reassuringly before I snatched the bottle of saline from the counter and used it to get Gloria as clean as possible.

I'd kill for some betadine at the moment, but I was grateful for the items Ralph had gotten for me.

"Can I help with anything?" Millie questioned from behind me.

"I could really use a clean baby blanket or some towels. Preferably both," I answered without taking my eyes off Gloria's progress.

"I'll find them," Millie said determinedly before she left the booth.

I took a deep breath and let it out, knowing this baby was going to be here before anyone was ready for it.

I was just praying that whoever was driving that ambulance had a lead foot.

Chapter 14

Reese

Gloria's baby girl was born with a few gentle pushes and about fifteen seconds before the paramedics arrived.

I was relieved to see some equipment and to get their assistance. We all completed the rest of the things that needed to be done together, and I was so grateful when there were no signs of post-delivery complications.

Once Gloria and the baby were bundled up on the gurney one of the paramedics asked, "Do you want to ride with us, Reese? You're a much higher license than we are."

I shook my head regretfully. "I'm not licensed in the state of Montana. I was just helping because it was an emergency. I'm technically just a good Samaritan."

"You're one hell of a good Samaritan," the medic joked. "And you're still welcome to come along."

I nodded at the father of the baby. "I think you'd better take Tim. He still looks pretty anxious."

"I have two kids," he said with a chuckle. "It took me days to get over the deliveries, and I'm in the medical field. It's different when the patient is your family. The wife handled it better than I did."

I handed the paramedic the phone number I'd written on a piece of paper. "If anyone has questions about the delivery, please tell them to feel free to give me a call. And if you wouldn't mind, can you text me to let me know that all went well on the transport and that Gloria is at the hospital? I might not be licensed here, but I'd just like to know that she's where she needs to be to get checked over."

He nodded. "You got it."

I stood and watched as the ambulance drove out of the park.

"That was a little scary, right?" Hannah said from behind me. "You were amazing, Reese."

I turned to look at her. "I'm so sorry, Hannah. I know I have some explaining to do, but I'd like to go home and clean up first."

"We're taking you," Anna said as she joined Hannah. "Once you're done, we're all meeting at Millie's place. She's worried. I think the family needs to be in on this discussion."

"Where's Devon?" I asked. "I came here with him."

"He's helping Kaleb and Tanner with cleanup. They'll meet us at Millie's place. We told him we were taking you home for a shower and a stiff drink. Ralph insisted on being at the meeting, too."

I nodded solemnly. "I think he should be there."

I still couldn't believe that I'd blown my cover, but I could hardly risk the life of a mother and child if I could help in some way.

I'd rather risk my own life than the lives of a mother and child.

The delivery had gone well for a precipitous delivery, but the cord had been wrapped around the baby's neck, and that could have gotten ugly if no one was around with enough experience to fix it.

I'd make the same decision all over again.

However, I was about to face the consequences of my actions, and it wasn't going to be pleasant.

The ladies talked about the delivery while I was showering and putting on clean clothing, but they didn't ask me any questions.

Hannah simply handed me a shot of something that looked like hard liquor before we left my apartment, and I tossed it back without a single hesitation.

I knew it was false courage…but it was something.

I wasn't quite sure how I was going to look at the faces of the people who meant the most to me in this town and explain to them why I'd been lying to them since the moment I'd set foot in Crystal Fork.

"It looks like the gang is all here," Anna commented as she surveyed all of the vehicles in front of Millie's house. "I hope you don't mind, Reese, but Lauren is here, too."

I turned and sent her a weak smile. "She's family. She deserves to know."

Anna hopped out of the back seat as soon as the vehicle stopped and headed toward the house, but Hannah put a gentle hand on my arm before I could exit.

"Wait, Reese," she entreated, not making a single move to get out of her car. "I don't know what's going on, but I want you to know that I'll never stop being your friend. I know you. If you were hiding who you really are, there's a reason for it."

"There is," I told her as tears filled my eyes. "But that doesn't change the fact that I've been lying to everyone."

"And it's been eating you alive," Hannah commented. "I suspected something wasn't right, but I didn't want to invade your privacy. I knew you'd tell me when you were ready."

I swiped a tear from my cheek. "You'll probably never know how hard it's been not to share everything with the people I care about here."

"Just tell me one thing," she requested. "Was your life in danger?"

I nodded slowly.

"Then I really don't give a shit if you told me a thousand lies, Reese," she said adamantly. "Your safety comes first."

"I really do have a business degree," I blurted out. "I minored in business in college. I just don't have the experience in business that's on my resume."

"You've saved my ass many times at Glam Anywhere. Do you really think I care about that piece of paper or your experience," Hannah scolded. "You've help me a lot, Reese. Now let me help you. Let's get the truth out, and then you'll tell me how I can help. *Shesh!* No wonder you were an expert on pregnancy. I not only had a talented, creative manager, but a healthcare expert at my disposal. You've helped me a lot during this pregnancy."

I shrugged. "It's what I do."

"This isn't going to be an inquisition, Reese. I want you to know that. We just want to know how we can help. Let's go before you make this out to be worse than it really is."

As soon as we exited the vehicle, Hannah came to me and put her arms around me in a very reassuring, caring hug.

I hugged her back, closing my eyes as I savored the warmth of her friendship.

I felt so damn lucky to have a friend like Hannah in my life.

No questions asked about my situation, she trusted me, even though I'd given her no reason to do so.

When we entered the house, everyone was already seated around Millie's large dining room table that she rarely used unless she had company.

My gaze locked with Devon's almost immediately, but his expression was guarded, so I couldn't read a single thing he was thinking at the moment.

Hannah plopped into a chair next to Tanner, and I took the only seat left between Millie and Devon.

Ralph, who was sitting directly across from me commented, "The first thing I'm going to request is that none of the information shared here goes outside of this group. I've already contacted Tim and told him that Reese's life depends on him not sharing the information he got today. He's grateful to Reese, and he promised they'd never say a word."

I relaxed a little as I realized that Ralph was going to direct and lead the conversation so I didn't have to do it.

He continued. "I'm going to tell you the situation, but I'm going to leave it up to Reese about how much she wants to share about her personal life with all of you. The two of us met in Spokane a year ago. I was the lead detective on the murder of her business partner and her own attempted murder. The perpetrator was a disgruntled patient who had lost his wife and child during a delivery. Reese was a labor and delivery nurse at the time, and her partner, an OB physician, was the delivering doctor. It was a tragedy, but they did everything they could do to save those lives during that delivery. The perp lost his mind over a year later, entered the medical office they were working in, and shot both Reese and the physician. Reese's partner and friend didn't survive the shooting. Apparently, when the disgruntled husband found out that Reese was still alive, he came to the hospital and tried to make sure she died. Luckily, she had around-the-clock protection in the hospital, and the man fled and hasn't been seen since. Once she recovered, she needed to be protected and hidden until he was apprehended, but US Marshall's are still searching for him. I'd already taken this job in Crystal Fork, so I suggested to a friend at the US Marshall's office that this town would be a good place for her to lay low for a while. She's not officially in the WITSEC program, but it wasn't difficult to get her a new identity. We never imagined it would take us this long to find this asshole."

"Has he made contact with her since he tried to kill her at the hospital?" Kaleb asked gruffly.

"He's attempted to contact her several times via her old identity. We monitor all of her old digital information, and this asshole wants her dead. She needs to stay hidden. If he finds out her new identity, he'd kill her in a heartbeat. He's out of his mind. We've gotten close to apprehending him, but he gets tipped off somehow and leaves right before we get to his location."

"How badly was she injured?" Hannah asked in a tearful tone.

Ralph looked at me and I nodded. I had no hesitation about answering any of the questions people wanted to ask.

Now that the truth was out, there wasn't going to be any further lies or evading questions for me.

"The bullet barely missed her heart," Ralph answered. "She needed emergency surgery to save her life, and she was in the hospital for a while. She can tell you any of the details she chooses to share. I will say this…I've grown fond of Reese, and I'll do anything I can to protect her. She's been through hell and is still going through hell. She lost a friend and a partner and almost lost her own life. She was tossed into this situation through no fault of her own. If you have a problem with her lying to all of you, put yourself in her place. She left everyone and everything she loved to come to this place with nobody but me to talk to about it. The agreement when her new identity was created was that she tells absolutely no one the truth. If anyone has a problem with that, you come to me. Reese has been through enough."

"Nobody is going to give her any grief," Tanner rumbled. "They'd have to go through me first."

Ralph sent Tanner a satisfied smile. "Glad you see it my way."

"I know we all do," Millie commented. "I don't think anyone can imagine being in her situation, but all of the Remingtons will be here for her. And not a single one of us will ever reveal her secret. We understand how important that is now."

"That's about all of the facts I'm going to give you," Ralph said in a firm tone. "You know what you need to know. It's up to Reese how much she wants to share about her real life."

"It's really all we need to know," Tanner agreed. "We'll all be there to protect her whenever she needs it. Is she safe in her apartment alone?"

"As safe as she can be," Ralph replied. "She has nosy neighbors that always have their eyes out for trouble of any kind."

"She can stay with us," Hannah said adamantly.

I almost jumped out of my chair when Devon slammed his fist down on the table. "Fuck that! She's staying with *me*. Nobody has to protect her. If that asshole wants her dead, he'd have to kill me first, and that's not going to happen."

He stood, took my hand, and pulled me to my feet.

"We're leaving," he announced. "Reese has had enough for one day. You can ask all of the rest of your questions later."

Without another word, he pulled me by my hand toward the door and never looked back.

And because I was shocked, I let him lead me out the door without a single protest.

If he'd stopped for just a single second and turned around, he would have seen all of the approving faces of his family still sitting around the dining room table.

Chapter 15

Devon

We were at my house in less than thirty minutes. I'd stopped at Reese's apartment, and I told her to gather what she needed for a few days.

We'd get the rest of her stuff later.

She'd tried to argue that she was fine in her apartment.

I told her she wasn't, and if she didn't grab her stuff that I'd do it for her, and she might not end up with everything she needed.

She'd come back ten minutes later with a small suitcase that I'd tossed in the back of my truck.

I handed her a glass of wine after we'd gotten into my family room, and she'd settled herself on the sofa. I sat beside her with something a little stronger.

I took a deep breath. "You can talk or not talk," I rumbled. "I'm good just knowing you're here and that you're safe."

I should have been there for her after Gloria and her newborn had left in the ambulance.

I hadn't because I'd been too busy sulking about the fact that she hadn't told me that she was a completely different woman than the one I'd come to know.

I'd thought that I'd needed some space for a while to try to digest the fact that Reese…wasn't really Reese.

Now, I wanted to kick myself for being such an asshole.

My gut twisted at the thought of her nearly dying because some lunatic shot her.

Never, during all of the time that I'd wanted to know her secrets, did it occur to me that she could have suffered that much or that she was in that much danger.

I was pissed off and furious, but none of that was directed at Reese.

She'd had no choice but to keep silent.

I was angry with myself.

"I'm sorry," she said quietly. "I wanted to tell you the truth so badly, but I couldn't. I agreed to the terms when I was offered a new identity."

"Don't ever be sorry for protecting your own life," I growled. "I hate the shit you've been through, Reese. Is your name really Reese?"

She nodded. "Catherine Reese Monroe. I've always gone by Reese. I'm the same woman you've always known, Devon. I've never lied to you about who I am as a person. I'm the same nerd that I've always been. I'm thirty-two, not twenty-eight. My age and birthdate needed to be changed."

"You're still young," I grumbled.

"I almost slipped a few times and said that I started watching my diet more closely once I hit my thirties. We got so close, and I got so comfortable with you that it was hard not to make little mistakes once in a while. What else do you want to know?"

"Tell me about your real career," I suggested. "Why a nurse practitioner?"

"Both of my parents are doctors. I guess it came naturally. I thought about going to medical school, but I found myself more drawn toward nursing. You get more of a personal connection with your patients. After a few years in labor and delivery, I decided to go back to school and become a nurse practitioner. After I finished, Kyle asked me to join his OB/GYN practice. He was an incredible physician, and I loved working with him in the hospital. We weren't just colleagues, we were friends. By the time I got certified, I'd worked with him in labor and delivery for years. It wasn't easy waking up from surgery and finding out that he didn't make it."

Fuck! I hadn't meant to bring up bad memories for her.

"You obviously liked your job," I mused. "How has it been working as an office manager when you're really a nurse practitioner."

"I minored in business," she explained. "So I really do have a business degree. I thought I might want to work in nurse management someday, so I thought the business degree might be helpful. I've never worked in a business office in my life. I didn't want to fail Hannah. That was my only concern. I actually enjoy working at Glam Anywhere, but I do miss my real profession."

"What do your parents and your friends think about all of this?" I asked curiously.

"They don't know," she said in a tremulous voice. "Nobody knows where I am. Them knowing could put them in danger, and any communication could be tracked. I haven't talked to anyone I love for months. That's probably the hardest part of all this. I used to talk to my mom almost every single day. She's probably worried sick about me. All I could say was that I was going away for a while to a safe place, and I'd contact them as soon as I was able. They don't know I'm living under a false identity in Crystal Fork, Montana. I never thought I'd have to be away from them this long without a single phone call."

It nearly gutted me when I saw the tears in her eyes.

I couldn't imagine not having some kind of contact with my family for months.

I could tell she was worried about her parents, and I understood that perfectly.

I took our glasses and put them on the coffee table so I could pull her against me and wrap my arms around her. "I'm not asking any more questions. I hate seeing you cry," I rasped against her hair.

The woman I was holding had been through so much pain and fear in the last year that I was surprised that she was still calm and sane.

"I'm okay," she murmured against my shoulder. "It's probably good for me. I've had to hold everything together for so long that I've probably never dealt with any of my emotional baggage. That meltdown in your kitchen was the only time I was ever able to lose it."

Reese's calmness in a situation like this one amazed me.

She might not be the greatest liar in the world, but her bravery and her ability to keep her head together after all she'd been through was a fucking miracle to me.

I tightened my arms around her. "Feel free to dump that baggage on me any time you want."

She smacked my arm playfully, "I wouldn't dump my baggage on my worst enemy, much less a friend." She paused before she asked in the same light tone, "What was that caveman act you pulled at my apartment tonight?"

"I wasn't coming home without you," I said simply. "You *are* staying here with me."

"You're doing it again," she pointed out.

"I'm not fucking around with your safety, Reese. I don't use it often, but I have an excellent security system here, and we'll be using it all the time from now on. I'm also getting you a protection trained dog as soon as I can find one."

"Do you want a dog?" she asked curiously.

"I've always had one. I lost my fourteen-year-old female border collie a year ago. I haven't had the heart to replace her. Now I'm ready for another dog."

"Because you want to protect me?" she questioned suspiciously.

"Yep." I wasn't going to lie to her. I liked having a dog, but my motivation to get one revolved around Reese's safety right now.

"Don't do it," she warned. "I'll use the security system. I'm not letting you get a dog just to protect me. I'm here willingly. I didn't fight you about coming here because I always feel safer when I'm with you. But I'm putting my foot down on this one."

"We'll see," I said noncommittally. I *had* gotten what I wanted now that she'd agreed to come stay with me. I didn't want to push my luck, but I wanted to keep my future protection possibilities open.

"I keep hoping all of this will be over soon," Reese murmured. "I've been terrified since the day Burke burst into our medical office. It's been like a nightmare that never ends."

"Are you still scared?" I asked her.

She took a deep breath. "I hate to admit it, but almost all the time. I'm always hyper aware of my surroundings and looking over my shoulder. Rationally, I know that Crystal Fork is a safe place and that I'm well-hidden here under a new identity, but I'm never quite comfortable. I'm probably the most relaxed when I'm here with you."

That was probably incredibly normal when you knew there was someone out there who wanted you dead. No matter how well she'd been hidden.

"I'm always a little edgy," she continued. "I hate the sound of gun-shots or anything that sounds like one, and I still have nightmares occasionally about the shooting. I probably still have a little PTSD that I've never been able to deal with because I can't talk to anyone."

No wonder she hadn't wanted to learn how to use a gun.

It was a helpless feeling for me to know that Reese needed some help coping with her past trauma but couldn't get the help she needed.

"Until you can get some trauma counseling, talk to me," I insisted. "I can't give you much advice, but I can listen. You have someone other than Ralph to talk to now."

"I adore him," she shared. "He's done so much for me, but he is a no-nonsense kind of guy. He's not exactly someone I'd talk to about my trauma."

"You can tell me anything," I said, and I meant it.

If Reese needed me, I was going to be there for her.

"I guess I'm going to have to earn your trust back before we can truly be friends again," Reese mused.

"You don't owe me anything," I growled. "You did what you had to do for your safety. You never intentionally lied to me, Reese. I trust you, but I want to get to know you more now that everything is out in the open. I admire what you did for Gloria today. I didn't see it, but I could hear you from outside the booth. I didn't let Ralph chase me away. You were pretty calm when you decided their lives were more important than your safety. Doing a high-risk delivery in the middle of a park is pretty ballsy, but it never seemed to faze you. I don't know that part of you. We don't have to start over. I just want to get to know the parts of you that I don't know yet."

"I want that, too," she said with a small yawn.

I got up with her still in my arms. "You're tired. It's getting late. Let's get you to bed. It's been a long day for you."

Reese was probably exhausted emotionally and physically after what happened at the park and all of the talk about her past today.

From now on, I considered it my privilege to take care of Reese Monroe, and I was going to take that job very seriously.

"My bag," she said sleepily.

I scooped up the small suitcase I'd brought in and put it on her lap.

"You're not seriously going to carry me and this suitcase up all of those stairs," she said, alarmed.

I grinned at her. "Now that you said that I'm tempted to do it, but I do have an elevator that goes up."

"Use it, please," she said. "I don't want you to end up with a hernia."

For all her talk of extra pounds, Reese was a small woman, and she hadn't brought much with her. I could easily carry her up the steps, but I got into the elevator to make her happy.

"I've never seen the upstairs area of your home," she commented.

I found that interesting since she'd had every opportunity to look around while I was out of town.

"I'm putting you in the bedroom right next to mine," I informed her. "If you ever need me, I'm out the door and to the right."

"Thank you for this," she said quietly.

"You don't ever have to thank me for helping you, Reese. We're friends. It's what people do when they care about someone. You'd do the same for me."

"I guess I'm used to being the one who takes care of everyone else," she said thoughtfully.

"Then I guess it's about time someone took care of you for a change," I informed her as we arrived in her room.

As I put her gently on the bed, she suddenly lifted her head, her eyes wide open. "I never got to bid on the necklace at the auction!"

I dug into the pocket of my jeans. I was going to save the surprise for later, but she looked so disappointed that I wasn't about to make her wait.

I held up the necklace. "You mean this one?" I teased. "I had a friend win the bid for me. It's yours. Consider it a gift for all the times you've fed me."

"Devon, I have to pay you for it. I'm not sure I have enough in my savings here to cover it, but I have money I can't access in my real bank accounts."

"Not happening. I'm a billionaire, Reese. Just let me give you one small gift without being stubborn about it."

She took the necklace from me like it was a priceless diamond necklace.

"It's so beautiful," she said with a sigh. "But I'm not taking advantage of you just because you have billions of dollars. I'll take it, but only if you let me do something nice for you in return someday."

I could think of a million *nice* things she could do for me that would make me extremely happy, but I wasn't opening up that topic right now.

My priority was her well-being right now, and what she needed was some sleep.

The friends with benefits discussion that had gotten interrupted earlier was going to have to wait.

Now that I knew everything that she'd been through all I wanted to do was make sure that she felt...safe.

Chapter 16

Reese

The following week turned out to be the best days I'd ever spent in Crystal Fork.

Hannah had no problem with me continuing to work at Glam Anywhere even though I'd lied about my work experience. She'd insisted on me staying in my current job.

None of the Remington family treated me any differently than they had previously. In fact, they were even more protective and kind to me.

I'd answered all questions they wanted to ask about my life because I had nothing to hide with them anymore, and I wanted all of my friends to know the real me.

"How are things going living with Devon?" Hannah asked as we ate lunch together in the reception area of the office on Friday afternoon.

"He's been incredible," I answered honestly after I'd swallowed a bite of my chicken salad. "But he's definitely overprotective."

Devon took me to work every day after we got a coffee at The Mug And Jug, and he left work early to pick me up at closing time.

Never, at any time, was I alone at his place, and he was diligent about locking up the house and setting the alarm system.

Hannah snorted. "I think that's true of all of the Remington brothers and their women."

I looked at her in surprise. "I'm not his woman."

"Are you kidding?" she asked drily. "We all saw him lose his mind at Millie's when he found out what happened to you. And his behavior after that. Devon never acts like that. He definitely considers you his woman."

"We're not together, Hannah. We're friends. I'm not going to lie and say that I'm not attracted to him. No more lies of any kind with anyone who knows the truth from now on."

"He's obviously attracted to you, too," Hannah observed. "The two of you have never..."

"Had sex?" I finished for her since she'd probably stopped because she didn't want to invade my privacy. But I trusted Hannah and there wasn't much I wouldn't tell her. "Nope. You know that Devon doesn't do commitments or girlfriends. I'm so attracted to him that I even offered him a friends with benefits thing with no strings attached. He never really gave me an answer and he hasn't mentioned the topic this week."

"Probably because he wants more than that," Hannah answered. "And he's probably more focused on protecting you and helping you through this whole ordeal."

I nodded. "He has been really focused on my mental health because I told him I still have some PTSD from the shooting. I'm not sure how he pulled it off, but he actually found me a counselor that I started meeting with this week via video that wouldn't ask any questions or require any of my personal info. She specializes in treating people who've gone through a traumatic event in their lives. Kaleb asked his cousin Wyatt for a trauma specialist, and Wyatt knew somebody who would work with me, no questions asked. She seems really good at what she does, but it seems strange to me that she didn't even require my last name, address, or any of my personal data."

"According to Tanner, Wyatt has some mysterious connections, but he's not sure why," Hannah told me. "When Shelby was kidnapped and almost killed, there was zero media coverage of the event. Wyatt was able to kill the whole thing like it never happened. I think anyone he's recommending is safe."

"Devon said the same thing," I replied.

"Is there anything I can do to help?" Hannah queried. "I'm always here if you need to talk about it."

I shook my head. "I still have some nightmares about the shooting, and I panic when I hear anything that sounds like a gunshot, but I think this counselor can help with that. I guess I'm just starting to deal with it because everything is in the open now with all of you. Helping to deliver Gloria's baby was scary, too. In all of my years as a labor and delivery nurse, the only mother and baby I ever lost was Burke Kline's wife and child."

"What happened if you don't mind me asking?" Hannah questioned softly.

I'd already talked to Devon about that nightmare delivery, and I didn't mind sharing with Hannah.

"Her uterus ruptured before we could get her to surgery for a C-section. Something like that happening is pretty rare. Kyle and I were both devastated. Burke left the hospital, and we never saw him again until the shooting over a year later. It was actually my last delivery before I started as a nurse practitioner in Kyle's office. It was my last day as a labor and delivery nurse."

"What a horrible way to end your hospital career," Hannah said in a mortified voice.

"It was," I agreed. "I was actually glad that I didn't have to go back and help deliver more babies after that. I loved my job as a women's health NP. I helped Kyle with prenatal care for women, but I had a wide variety of things that I could do to help women of all ages."

"It must have been strange to switch to working in this office after spending most of your career in the hospital."

"Strange, but interesting," I shared. "I like what I'm doing here, Hannah. It's been a privilege to help get Glam Anywhere off the ground. In some ways, I'm still helping women. You're reaching so many women who are housebound and want those services. You're also making life easier for working women."

"I feel really good about that," Hannah agreed. "I love doing weddings and bridal stuff, but it's nice to branch out and be doing something else that I think is important."

"You're doing well in Montana," I pointed out. "Are you starting to think about going national?"

"Not until after our daughter is born," Hannah shared. "I'm thinking I'm going to need a new office manager once Burke Kline is apprehended. It's going to be hard to lose you. Are you going back to Spokane?"

"I haven't thought that far ahead," I said truthfully. "Probably. My parents are there, and we're close. But I can't say that I don't have amazing friends here now, too."

"You could stay and practice here," Hannah suggested. "Devon would be ecstatic. We all would be. Spokane isn't that far. He'd fly you to see your parents whenever you wanted."

"Devon might be happy to get me out of his home," I joked.

"I don't think so," Hannah answered. "I think he'd be crushed if you left. I've never seen Devon attached to a woman the way he's bonded with you, and he's been like a brother to me for a long time. He's crazy about you, and I mean that literally. He seems obsessed over your safety. I think you're underestimating how much he cares about you, Reese. I'm willing to bet that the pretty necklace you're wearing was a gift from Devon."

I fingered the beautiful turquoise and silver necklace around my neck as I answered, "He got someone to bid on it for him," I confessed. "I was going to bid on it at the auction myself, but I was busy trying to help deliver a baby."

"That was pretty thoughtful," Hannah observed. "And Devon isn't known for being that kind and considerate. He's changed since he met you, Reese."

I shook my head. "I think he's always been that way underneath all of his bluster," I said.

"The people who know and love him realize that," Hannah said. "But nobody else does."

"He has so many good qualities, and he's so creative," I mused. "I just wish I knew why he feels like it's necessary for most people to think he's kind of a jerk."

"If he ever decides to tell anyone, it will probably be you," Hannah answered. "Change of subject, but we're going to go to Billings on Sunday. Do you want to go? I know you're a little nervous about anyone recognizing you, but I could change your appearance. And Anna is an expert at disguise. I asked Ralph if it would be okay. He said if we can really change your appearance, it's up to you. I think he feels bad that you've never been able to get out of town. He might be a no-nonsense guy, but he cares about your mental well-being."

I let myself feel a little hopeful as I asked, "What can you change?"

There had been some publicity about the shooting, and my face had been in news articles nationally. That's why they'd kept me buried here in Crystal Fork. Going to a bigger town might have been risky.

"Just about everything," Hannah said confidently. "I can change your haircut and use some temporary hair color to take the red out of your hair. It will wash out so nobody in Crystal Fork will be suspicious. Anna has a variety of colored contact lenses now that she'd lend you to mask those distinctive eyes. She even has some that aren't prescription that she wears with her prescription glasses for an even better disguise. I'll even do your makeup before we leave."

I didn't wear a lot of makeup. Just enough to highlight my eyes and my lips.

Just the thought of feeling free enough to go a few places made my heart soar.

"Yes!" I squeaked excitedly. "Are we going shopping? There are so many things I'd like to get. I'm crocheting some things for your baby, but I really want to see the yarn in person, so I know it's exactly what I need."

I'd missed shopping in person, and I hadn't been able to do that in a very long time.

"We're absolutely shopping at the mall," Hannah said mischievously. "And eating. And gossiping. And getting a good massage. There's an expert in gentle massage for pregnant women at the spa. We always have so much fun on our days in Billings. I'm ecstatic that you can come with us. I'll be at Devon's place early on Sunday morning."

"Thank you, Hannah," I said as I forced back the tears that were threatening to fall. "This means a lot to me."

I'd felt confined for so long, and I wanted to do something that felt normal with the friends that I cared about.

"Don't expect Devon to be as thrilled as you are," Hannah warned. "He doesn't seem to want to let you out of his sight."

"I'll handle him," I said with a sigh. "I'd love to get him something in Billings because he snagged this beautiful necklace for me, but what do you get a billionaire who has everything?"

He probably wouldn't be happy about the outing, but he was going to have to realize that he couldn't protect me every minute of the day.

She winked at me. "If anyone can handle him, it's you. And I have the same problem getting things for Tanner. We'll stop at Crumbl Cookies before we go back to Crystal Fork. All three of our guys have a weakness for those cookies. Anna and I always bring a box home so our men stop sulking over us leaving for the day." She lifted a hand before I could speak. "And don't tell me that Devon isn't your guy. He is. You just don't realize it yet."

I gave up on that argument. Hannah was convinced that Devon cared about me in a girlfriend sort of way, and I wasn't going to convince her otherwise. "I was hoping for something a little nicer than cookies. He won't tell me how much he paid for the necklace, and he definitely won't take the money, but I'm sure it was pricey."

"When your man is a billionaire, it's the little things that mean a lot to them," Hannah explained. "Thoughtful things. Get some yarn and crochet him something he can use or something he can put on his wall. He'll like that more than you spending a bunch of money on him."

She was probably right. Money meant nothing to any of the Remington men because they had more of it than they could possibly spend in several lifetimes. Maybe that was why Devon had been so surprised and happy when I'd made him that hummingbird cake. He always seemed to appreciate things that I'd spent time to make for him.

Finished with lunch, Hannah and I dumped our containers and got back to work.

For the rest of the day, I racked my brain to try to think about something I could give Devon to make him feel special.

After all the things he'd done for me, he deserved it.

He'd made me feel safe.

He'd made me feel cared for and happy.

Those were all gifts that I wasn't quite sure how to repay.

Chapter 17

Devon

"**I** don't like it," I grumbled later that evening. "At all."
Then again, I didn't like anything that was going to put
Reese at risk in any way.

I knew she wanted to explore Billings and other areas of Montana,
and I wanted that for her, but my first instinct was to make sure
she was safe.

"If Hannah can disguise my appearance, it's not the least bit risky,"
she said in a voice meant to make me a little more rational as she put
our dinner in the oven.

"I still don't like it," I said unreasonably. "If you have to go, I'd
rather you were going with me."

"Do you really want to shop and get a massage?" she teased.

I had an assistant who did my shopping because I hated doing it
myself most of the time, and the only massage I wanted would have
to be performed by the woman I was looking at right now.

"No," I said honestly. "I want you safe."

Reese walked over to where I was leaning against the kitchen
counter. "I'll be perfectly safe."

B. A. Scott

"With three women, one of them pregnant?" I questioned. "None of you even carry a weapon."

"Not true," Reese said calmly. "Anna always carries pepper spray for her protection. And no one is going to recognize me. Hannah is going to change my appearance completely before we go. Even Ralph approved it. It's not like Burke Kline is going to be hanging out in Billings on the off chance that I might show up there. The main worry was someone recognizing me as that woman involved in that shooting in Spokane. That's not going to happen."

Hell, I still wasn't even used to the idea that Reese was from Spokane and not Salt Lake City.

Turns out, she'd never even been to Salt Lake City.

It was all part of her cover.

During the last week, I'd discovered that Reese was still...Reese.

Her occupation was different, and some of the facts I'd thought I'd known about her history were different, but she was still the same woman.

Unfortunately, she was also still just as stubborn as she'd been under her fake identity.

"If I tell you that you're not going, are you still going to do it?" I asked gruffly.

"Yes," she said in a truthful tone. "I care about your opinion, but I've run my own life for a long time, and I like it that way. I've already agreed not to ride alone until this is over. I've made some compromises. But you have no idea what it's been like for me to be confined to Crystal Fork. Not to be able to do anything isn't normal for me. I'm tired of being afraid, hopeless, and helpless. I want a little freedom for one damn day."

"I get that," I said irritably. "You want me to compromise this time. That's hard for me to do, especially when every instinct I have is telling me to protect your beautiful ass and not take any risks. I'm also not used to compromising when I want something."

She lifted a brow. "Do you always get your way?"

"Always, except when it comes to family."

"Then pretend that I'm the sister you never had," she said, sounding equally annoyed.

I crowded her against the counter and put one hand on each side of her so she couldn't escape. "That's pretty hard to do when all I can think about is getting you naked and fucking you until you can't think about anything else but me," I said huskily.

Christ! This woman was making me into a lunatic.

I wasn't entirely in control of my emotions when she was with me, and I fucking hated it. But I obviously didn't hate it enough to want her to be somewhere else.

Her annoyance seemed to disappear as our eyes locked, and the needy look in those gorgeous eyes made my control snap.

She needed me as much as I needed her, and that knowledge completely gutted me.

I speared my hand into her hair and jerked her mouth to mine.

The kiss wasn't gentle and coaxing.

It was full-on lust and carnality, but it was exactly what we both needed.

Reese Monroe was mine, and I wanted her to be aware of that fact in a way that was beyond just some kind of compulsion.

I felt her body yield.

I knew exactly when she stopped thinking about anything else but me and the heat that flowed between the two of us.

She wrapped her arms possessively around my neck and her short nails dug into my nape.

I welcomed the twinge of pain because I wanted her to be greedy.

I felt exactly the same way.

I shoved my hands under the oversized shirt she was wearing and stroked my hand over her soft skin.

I'd already discovered that Reese had a habit of not wearing a bra when she was at home, and I was damn glad there was nothing in the way of me being able to touch all of that soft, warm skin.

I let her come up for air, and I buried my face in her neck, tasting every inch of skin I could get my mouth on.

"Devon," she panted as I nipped at her neck.

Fuck! I loved hearing her say my name in that desperate tone.

One of my hands found its way to those beautiful breasts I'd only admired from afar until this very moment.

Her nipples were as hard as diamonds, and I knew she felt the sensation clear to her toes when I tweaked one of them.

"Oh, God," she cried out as her head fell back to give me access to anything I wanted.

"Devon," she crooned in a sultry voice that made my gut twist, and my cock beg to get inside her voluptuous body.

Not going to happen. Not yet.

I gripped the bottom of her shirt, pulled it over her head, and tossed it onto the floor so I could see exactly what I was fingering.

I'd never thought of myself as a boob guy, but the moment I laid eyes on Reese half naked; I was instantly obsessed with the most gorgeous tits I'd ever seen.

"You're so fucking beautiful, Reese," I growled right next to her ear before I covered one of those spectacular breasts with my mouth.

It was an awkward angle because I was so much taller than she was, but my mouth and teeth tormented those gorgeous breasts until Reese was moaning and squirming under my touch.

"Devon!" she cried out. "I need—"

"You need me to make you come. Say it, Reese," I demanded, wanting to hear her admit it out loud.

"Yes," she screamed as her nails dug hard into the skin of my neck. "Please."

Her entire body was trembling with need, and my gut ached from the desire to feel her and watch her come.

I slid my hand down beneath the stretchy, loose shorts she was wearing until I'd breached her panties and stroked over her pussy.

"You're so wet, Reese," I rasped against her neck.

She was so slick and hot that my cock jerked in reaction.

I ignored it, my entire focus on Reese and her pleasure.

"Fuck me," she pleaded in a voice that I almost couldn't resist.

"Don't think," I said as I nipped her earlobe. "Just feel, Reese."

Her breaths were coming hard and fast, and I savored the feel of that heat hitting my skin.

She was so aroused.

She was so damn beautiful.

And this woman was all mine.

I teased that slick pussy in a way that I knew would make her crazy. I used my fingers to fuck her and almost groaned when I felt how tightly her sheath gripped my fingers.

I stroked over her clit with my thumb, priming her beautiful body for what I knew was coming.

I lifted my head to watch her face.

Her skin was glowing with a light layer of perspiration, and her eyes were closed.

"Look at me, Reese," I commanded. "I want you to know exactly who's about to make your body explode."

"Devon," she said on a lusty moan as she opened those emerald eyes and caught my gaze.

The trust and adoration in her eyes were like a gut punch to me, and it instantly forced me to give her exactly what she needed.

I put pressure on her clit and stroked hard and fast until I could feel her entire body shaking uncontrollably as she orgasmed.

Hard.

The primal satisfaction I got from watching her fall apart was almost foreign to me, but I knew it was going to be addictive.

When she screamed my name over and over as her climax went on and on, I knew that was a sound I was going to want to hear a million times or more in the future.

I'd never get enough of it.

I'd never get enough of seeing her just like this.

I covered her mouth with mine as she crashed back down to Earth.

She kissed me back with so much passion that it made my chest ache.

That probably should have scared the hell out of me, but it didn't.

Everything…fucking everything was different with Reese and I wasn't shying away from those differences like I had earlier in our relationship.

She made me feel things that I never had before, but I was starting to realize that truly feeling alive was better than guarding every single emotion I had.

When I released her mouth, I simply held her tight until she recovered.

I couldn't say that I didn't want more, but I was content just to hold her warm body against mine knowing that she was satisfied.

"You didn't want to…" she said hesitantly against my shoulder, trailing off at the end.

"Fuck you?" I asked hoarsely. "Have my cock buried so deeply in your beautiful body that I couldn't think straight? Hell yes, I wanted it, but we need to talk first, and I wanted to watch you get off. My dick can wait."

"What do we need to talk about? Are you okay?" she asked, instantly sounding concerned about me.

Christ! That was one of the things that I adored about Reese.

If she thought something wasn't right with me, she immediately wanted to know because she cared about me.

"I'm fine," I said as I reached down and picked up her shirt and helped her get it back on her body. "I was going to try to explain at the fundraiser, but we were interrupted. I can't do a friends with benefits thing with you, Reese."

She looked crestfallen, and I knew I was going to have to explain a lot of things that I'd never told anyone before, not even my own family.

Chapter 18

Reese

Okay, I couldn't say that I wasn't disappointed, but I gave Devon a lot of credit for speaking his truth.

He obviously didn't want me as much as I wanted him, and I was going to have to be alright with that.

Unfortunately, my heart still ached, especially after what had just happened between the two of us.

"I understand," I said as I stepped back.

"No, I don't think you do," Devon said huskily as he moved forward, picked me up, and carried me into the family room.

He put me down on the sofa, sat next to me and wrapped his arm around me, pulling me close before he spoke. "You can't be a hookup for me, Reese. I care way too much about you for that, but I'm also not sure how to be your guy. I haven't been anyone's man since college, and that relationship soured my desire to have any kind of relationship with a woman for a very long time. I honestly didn't think I'd ever want that again."

"Are you going to tell me what happened?" I queried gently.

I wasn't quite sure where all of this was leading, but I sensed that it was important.

No, it was probably *beyond* important. I was fairly certain I was about to discover why there had always been two sides of Devon. One that was kind of a jerk and another that was the kindest man I'd ever known.

He finally nodded. "It was a really long time ago. I was in my last year at the university. I dated in high school and college, but I'd never fallen hard for anyone until I met Claudia. I thought she was a student. In the end I found out she wasn't. She was a con artist that just happened to be at the college when we met. All of the details aren't that important since it happened so long ago, but I was a total idiot. Our parents set all of us up with a large college fund to use while we were in school. I barely touched it until I met her. I wanted to make my own way and pay for most of my college expenses by working my way through school. She always needed something. Tuition. Money for things she needed to pay. A new vehicle. I gave her everything until I had nothing left to give her. It was a very short relationship. She managed to drain me dry in a very short period of time. But I was really infatuated, and she was incredibly good at making me feel like I mattered to her. Honestly, I was a stupid, naïve kid who didn't know the difference between love and extreme infatuation. I felt like an idiot when I found out that she was just trying to get everything she could from me. I also felt stupid that I'd never realized that she was quite a few years older than I was. She already had a boyfriend who was in a gang. After she dumped me because I had nothing left to give her, her boyfriend found me in a deserted location and tried to kill me because he didn't want me to go to the police."

I took his hand and squeezed it tightly. "What happened?"

He grinned down at me. "He obviously didn't succeed because I'm still alive and talking to you. I fought back and managed to get out of the situation with a few stab wounds that were fixed up in the emergency room with a lot of sutures."

"Oh, God, Devon," I said, horrified. "You could have been killed."

"I wasn't," he said nonchalantly. "But that incident taught me a lesson. I've never wanted to get serious with a woman since that day."

"You never told anyone? Not even your brothers?"

"I felt like a complete loser. I still do," he explained. "I never wanted anyone to know. I fell for a con. My brothers were already working to be successful in New York. It took me a long time to get over the fact that I'd fallen for a stupid con and almost died because of it. I was bitter and cynical after that. I never completely trusted a woman again after that happened. I just shut down emotionally. I figured I was better off staying out of relationships, and I've been perfectly okay with that decision…until I met you."

God, he'd been scared to trust any relationship after that, and I couldn't say that I blamed him.

He had put up so many walls that no woman ever had a chance of reaching the real Devon again.

It made me so angry that any woman could do that to a young man that had just wanted her to love him.

I remembered being in college and how naïve and unworldly I'd been at the time.

He'd been vulnerable prey for a greedy con woman.

"Now," he continued. "I want more for us, but I'm not sure how to be a good boyfriend or even if that's what you want, too."

Tears filled my eyes, and my heart ached for Devon.

He was making himself completely vulnerable to me right now, and I knew how hard that had to be for him.

He'd been alone for so long because he'd been too afraid to trust his own judgment when it came to romantic relationships.

"I want it to be real, too," I told him truthfully. "You're already a good man, Devon. You'd be an incredible boyfriend. Nothing that happened to you was your fault. You were young. I was pretty stupid when I was in my early twenties. We think we know everything, but we really know absolutely nothing about the world yet. What happened to the bitch who did this to you and her boyfriend?"

"They were both picked up the next day on another case. I wasn't their first victim, but I was the last. The last I knew, he was in jail for life for murder, and she was put away for a long time on multiple charges."

I nodded. "Good. Although that's kind of a shame because I'd like to punch her in the face myself."

His grin widened. "Are you becoming *my* protector now? I thought you were a healer."

"Not when somebody hurts someone I care about," I said fiercely. "It pisses me off."

"It was a long time ago, Reese. The incident doesn't matter anymore."

"It matters," I argued. "It left a very good man with emotional scars."

"I think I'm looking at the woman who can heal those completely," Devon said huskily. "I trust you, Reese, and I never thought I'd say that to a woman ever again."

A tear plopped onto my cheek. "That's probably the greatest gift anyone has ever given me. I trust you, too."

Given his history, it almost seemed like a miracle.

"Speaking of trust," he said sheepishly. "I have a confession to make since I want to make sure that I'm always honest with you from now on. You were right not to trust my motives in the very beginning. Originally, I had planned to get you into a more comfortable place to find out what you were hiding. That plan got derailed fairly quickly when I realized that you'd never do anything to hurt my family. It didn't take me long to realize that I'd been a total idiot, and that you were an incredible woman that I wanted to get to know because I liked you. I've been attracted to you since that first night at your apartment."

That wasn't exactly surprising to me. I'd always suspected his motives in the beginning, but what developed after that was definitely real for both of us.

I could hardly fault him for trying to protect the people he loved.

I *had* been lying to everyone, so his intuition had been right.

Even though I hadn't always been honest with him, he trusted me, and I'd die before I ever betrayed that trust in any way ever again.

"I'm glad you told me," I said softly. "But I really don't care what your motives were in the beginning. I was hiding things, and you didn't know me. You were just trying to protect your family. Your protectiveness is one of the things that I adore about you."

"So are you willing to give this a shot?" he asked in a serious voice. "I'll definitely screw up, and I probably won't do all of the things I should for you. I'm going to be incredibly inept with the relationship thing, but I promise that I'll try."

I reached up and stroked his stubbled jawline. "Oh, Devon, you're already more amazing than you know. We'll take it slow. You know I haven't had the best track record with boyfriends, so I'm no expert on good relationships."

"I think I can do better than those idiots," he rumbled. "They obviously didn't know a good woman when they had one."

Devon was at least a million times better than any guy I'd ever dated.

I wished he could understand that, but he apparently was worried about his lack of experience at being in a romantic relationship.

"I know a good man when I see one now," I murmured as I kissed his jawline.

"I'm not going to press you about a future," Devon commented. "I don't know what's going to happen when all of this is over for you. I just want to be with you with everything in the open. It's getting pretty damn hard pretending we're just friends. My family definitely isn't buying it."

I laughed. "I can tell you that Hannah definitely isn't."

"My mom and my brothers aren't fooled, either," Devon admitted. "We don't have to sleep together, Reese. You deserve some dates first, and some boyfriend behavior."

I wanted to argue after having a little taste of what it would be like to be with Devon, but I didn't.

I was going to let him take this at his own pace.

"What did you have in mind," I asked curiously. "We're riding together tomorrow. Is that a date?"

"If I had my way, I'd take some time off work and fly you any-where you wanted to go, but that's not possible right now. I'll think of something. You'll also be getting endless gifts, and you can't argue if they're coming from your man."

I sent him a warning look. "Please don't get crazy."

"Sweetheart," he said rationally. "I'm a billionaire. I have so much money that I don't know what to do with it, and I *am* going to give you things."

"I don't need anything," I argued. "I only have a small savings here, but I have money in my real accounts, and I'm the only child of wealthy parents. They aren't billionaire wealthy, but I'm their only child, and they spoil me rotten."

"Then it's my turn to spoil you rotten," Devon said adamantly. "That's my job now."

"And what exactly can I do for you?" I asked.

"You already spoil me," he said firmly. "You cook for me, you make me special things, and you care about me and not my money. Those things have meant a lot to me, Reese. A guy couldn't want anything more than that. This guy doesn't."

"Mind blowing sex?" I suggested in a sultry voice.

"Don't start on that, woman," he growled. "Or you'll never get a single date before you end up in my bed."

I wanted to tell him that it was just fine with me if he wanted to go that route, but he obviously had his mind made up about exactly how all of this should go.

"It's not easy to keep quiet about it," I said teasingly. "Not when you're about to date the hottest guy on the planet." I paused before I asked in a more serious voice, "You obviously saw my scar from the shooting. Is it still ugly? I try not to look at it."

"It's not ugly," he said like he was irritated that I thought that it was. "It's part of you, Reese, and every part of you is beautiful. It is a little scary how close it was to your heart, and it guts me to think about how much pain it caused you, but nothing about you will ever be ugly to me."

Sometimes Devon said the sweetest things that he didn't even know were sweet.

My hand went to the healed wound on my chest automatically. "I'm hoping it will fade, eventually."

Devon took my hand and removed it from my chest, holding it tightly. "It's a testament that you're a survivor, sweetheart. I'll show you my scars if it makes you feel any better. I have plenty of them. We all have scars."

I wiggled my brows. "Does that mean you'd have to take off your clothes to show them to me? If so, I'm all for that idea. I'd love to examine every one of them."

Devon let out a bark of laughter. "You're a wicked woman, Reese Monroe."

"Only with you," I told him with a sigh as I laid my head on his shoulder. "I guess I should check on dinner. It should be done soon. It's your turn to pick a movie to watch, but I am not watching The Matrix or The Shawshank Redemption again. Pick something else."

Unfortunately, I was all caught up on Antiques Roadshow.

Devon and I traded back and forth on picking movies to watch before bed every night.

He had a few that he could watch over and over if I let him.

Most of them were older classics that were definitely 'guy' movies.

"Die Hard?" he asked hopefully.

"We just saw that one earlier in the week," I complained jokingly as I got off the sofa to go rescue our dinner.

"Then I'll just let you pick," he said magnanimously as he stood. "I'm happy just being with you. I really don't care what we watch."

My heart somersaulted inside my chest.

God, this man really did say things that made me adore him even more.

I walked over to him, put my arms around his neck, and told him, "We'll watch Die Hard."

He kissed me until my entire body almost melted.

The embrace was slow, sexy, and adoring.

"Why?" he asked when he finally lifted his head.

"Because I'm happy just being with you, too," I confessed.

He shot me a shit-eating grin and then kissed me again.

The kiss was so thorough that our dinner was almost overcooked, but neither one of us cared.

Chapter 19

Devon

Reese and I ended up not watching a movie at all.

She'd asked if we could go to the music room so she could listen to me play, and I'd happily gone along with that suggestion.

I'd played a variety of music for her, and I'd worked with her on an easier duet on the piano.

She hadn't seriously played for a long time, but she still had her musical skills, and she loved music.

She'd caught on pretty quickly, and we'd spent an incredibly fun evening joking around at the piano. She'd gone to bed a while ago, but I was lying in my bed restless as hell.

I had no idea how I was going to manage to keep my sanity and keep my hands off of Reese until she had the kind of dating experience she deserved.

I'd just gotten myself off in the shower before bed, and I was still edgy.

I wanted her in a way I'd never wanted another woman before in my entire life.

She'd smelled like strawberries tonight.

I'd recently learned that she had a weakness for a particular brand of body mists that were lighter than typical perfumes or cologne. She always smelled like some kind of fruit or flowers.

For some reason, those scents did it for me more than any expensive women's perfumes I'd ever inhaled.

Maybe because those scents suited Reese so well, and I never knew what fresh scent she was going to be wearing on any particular day.

I'd already decided I was going to find out where I could buy them and get her every scent that existed so she could try them all.

It was a stormy night, and we had a line of severe thunderstorms that were rolling through.

I was used to Montana storms, but even I winced a little at a large crack of thunder that sounded right over the house.

"Devon?" Reese's nervous voice called from my bedroom door.

I sat up immediately. "What's wrong?"

"That was loud. Do you think the horses are okay?"

The horses were fine.

I'd checked on them all and made sure they were comfortably in their stalls in the barn because I knew the storms were due to hit.

But I had to wonder if Reese was okay.

That thunder had almost sounded like a loud explosion, and I knew she didn't like that kind of noise.

"They're fine. They're used to the storms around here," I assured her. "Are you okay?"

"Honestly, I hate the explosive thunder. I used to love thunderstorms. Now I hate them. Can I stay with you for a few minutes?"

I only had the light from a small reading light on my nightstand, but I didn't have to see her clearly to know that she was uneasy. I could hear it in her voice.

"Come here," I said as I held my arms open for her.

She sprinted to the bed, climbed under the covers, and leapt into my arms.

Fuck! It felt good to have her come to me and to trust me to protect her.

"I'll just stay until the storm passes," she assured me in a relieved voice as she wrapped her arms around my neck tightly.

I flopped back onto my pillow and pulled her with me until she was half laying on my chest.

I had her in my bed.

I certainly wasn't about to complain.

She could stay as long as she liked.

I stroked my hand over her hair soothingly as the storm raged outside. "What did you do during other thunderstorms?"

"I've never been through one quite this bad since I got here," she said. "I just sucked it up."

That was probably true. Our thunderstorms could get pretty ugly at this time of year, but she hadn't been here at this time last year. Our storms had been fairly mild at the end of the summer and fall of last year.

We hadn't had a thunderstorm directly over the town that was this fierce in quite some time.

Her body was trembling a little as another loud crack of thunder shook the house.

"I hate this," she said angrily. "I hate being afraid of something that I never was before. I used to love a good thunderstorm rolling in."

She was frustrated.

I could hear it in her voice.

Reese was a strong woman, and it was evident that she hated these involuntary responses because of her trauma.

"It will go away, Reese. It's your body's response to previous trauma. You've never had a chance to deal with the PTSD from the shooting. Be patient with yourself."

"I'm trying," she said in a calmer voice. "Are the horses really not afraid of storms like this? I keep thinking about Luna."

"Some horses are scared of thunderstorms," I admitted. "Horses are like any other animal. Some react and some don't. Luckily, none of mine are that reactive to storms. Especially if they're inside and they feel safe. Luna is a trooper. She's never been that bothered by storms."

I felt her body relax a little.

"Thank God," she answered. "I don't like the thought of her being afraid."

Reese had gotten incredibly attached to Luna, and Luna to Reese. "I was going to save this until tomorrow, but I think you could use a distraction right now. Luna is yours, Reese. I want you to have her. The two of you belong together. I can't officially change ownership right now because you're under an assumed name, but I will after all of this is over."

The distraction obviously worked, because her eyes widened and the apprehension in her gaze disappeared.

"I can't just take an expensive horse from you," she protested. "I adore her, but I can't do it."

I grinned at her. "You're going to have to," I teased. "I think she's adopted you as her owner. She's bonded to you. You're her preferred person. She doesn't care about the rest of us anymore."

"I feel like I've bonded with her, too," Reese replied. "But I can't just take her from you."

"Yes, you can," I urged. "I never ride her because she's too small for me, and I have plenty of other horses. You love her. Admit it."

"I do," she whined. "And I'd love for her to be mine, but I've looked up prices on the breed. A horse with her bloodlines must have cost a fortune. And what about your mom? Luna was her horse."

"My mother would be thrilled if you took over ownership. She's happy that someone is loving on Luna and riding her every day because she can't anymore. It was hard for her to give her up, but she's more bonded to the horse she kept."

"Is it really possible that she could be mine just like that?" she said, her voice awed. "I need to pay you for her, Devon."

"Billionaire boyfriend, remember," I said playfully. "Your money is no good with me."

She slapped me on the arm. "Why do you have to be so stubborn? Luna is worth everything to me."

"And seeing you happy is worth everything to me," I countered. "Just take her as a gift and a favor to me."

I knew that Reese owned a small house in Spokane, and that she didn't have any property, but we'd figure that out later.

I was hoping she'd decide to stay in Montana.

Hell, I was counting on it because I didn't think I could do some kind of long-distance boyfriend thing with Reese.

It would kill me.

It wouldn't be impossible for me to relocate, but it would be pretty damn complicated with our offices in Billings.

I knew I was jumping ahead of myself because Reese and I didn't know what would happen with our relationship, but I knew I'd never be the one to break it off.

I couldn't imagine her not being part of my life anymore.

"Okay," she finally conceded. "This whole billionaire thing is going to be an adjustment for me. My parents have been good to me, but I'm not wealthy. I make a good salary, but I've always been on a budget. I refused to let them help me purchase my home. They're getting close to retirement, and they need to enjoy the money they worked so hard for over the years. I'd barely moved into my own home when this happened. I was so proud to be a homeowner on my own, but I never really got to enjoy it."

"All of this will be over soon, Reese. I know it's been dragging on forever, but Kline can't run from the authorities forever. He's gotten lucky a few times, but they'll get him."

"I keep telling myself the same thing," she said with a sigh. "I just hope he doesn't hurt anyone else before they do. One of the things I remember the most is the crazy look in his eyes before we were shot. His mind completely snapped. He was kind of an unpleasant guy, but he wasn't completely crazy before he lost his wife and child."

I rubbed my palm up and down her arm. "Are you feeling better? The storm is passing."

"Yeah, that was quite a distraction," she teased as she nipped at my ear. "There's only one other thing that would have distracted me more."

I gritted my teeth as she ran her hand over my bare chest and abdomen, exploring.

I was wearing a pair of sleep pants, but I never wore a shirt to bed.

She was wearing a pair of sleep shorts and a matching top that I'd seen before when she'd come down for coffee in the morning.

It wasn't meant to be sexy, but my dick got hard every time I saw her in that outfit, and tonight was no different.

Hell, my cock was hard every time she was in the same room with me, no matter what she was wearing.

"I'm not even going to ask what that distraction might be," I said firmly.

Fuck! This woman was making me completely insane.

I had a love/hate thing going on with her hands roaming all over my body.

I wanted her hands all over me, but it made it extremely difficult to leave mine off of her.

"You have an incredible body, Devon," she said as she stroked her hand over my abs.

Her tone was full of wonder, like she'd never felt a man's body before.

When she moved slightly lower, my patience had reached the end.

I flipped her onto her back and covered her body with mine. "You're asking for trouble, Reese," I growled. "A guy can only take so much."

Her face was immediately contrite. "I'm sorry. I shouldn't have done that. You just felt so good. I lost it for a moment. Let me get up. The storm is gone. I'll go back to my room. I know this isn't what you want right now."

She pushed hard against my shoulders with tears swimming in her eyes.

I was so stunned that I let her go.

What in the holy fuck had just happened?

She'd just fled the room like her gorgeous ass was on fire.

Not what I wanted?

I wanted her so badly that I was losing my shit.

I just wanted to do this relationship the right way, and I hadn't had a relationship since college.

I'd wanted to please her and treat her the way she deserved to be treated.

And in the process, I'd obviously hurt her somehow.

I'd just done something that I'd never wanted to do, and I wasn't even sure how it had happened.

Chapter 20

Reese

I swiped the tears from my cheeks as I crawled into my own bed.
What in the hell was I doing?
Devon had asked me for one thing…to wait a while before we
slept together.

I'd just pushed him to the point of anger, and I hated myself
for that.

He'd comforted me when I'd needed him, and then I'd gone and
made him mad because I'd insisted on pushing his boundaries.

Dammit! I'd never been the type of woman who had aggressively
gone after sexual gratification but being that close to Devon had
made me into a woman I never wanted to be.

I was needy and sexually frustrated.

But that was no damn excuse for ignoring what he wanted.

"What in the fuck just happened?" Devon asked in a graveled
voice after he'd pushed the door of my bedroom open. "And why in
the hell are you crying?"

"I'm mad at myself," I told him as I sat up and crossed my arms
over my chest. "You told me that you wanted to wait, and I totally

ignored that request. You make me crazy. You're ridiculously hot, and you were in bed with no shirt on. I couldn't keep my hands off you. I've never been like this."

"Like what?" he said as he raised a brow.

"A horny, pushy female who can't keep her hands off a guy. I'm turning into someone I've never been before, and I hate it. I've never been an incredibly sexual woman. I'm not some kind of femme fatale who tries to tempt some guy into having sex. But I act like one whenever I'm with you. It has to stop. I need to start listening to my brain again, but you make it into mush."

"There's a few problems with that," he said as he strolled toward the bed.

"What problems?" I asked.

He folded his arms across his stupidly broad, muscular chest. "Number one...I'm not *some* guy, I'm *your* guy, and you should feel free to touch me whenever you want. Number two...I happen to love the fact that you want me. Number three...we're in a relationship, Reese, and as weird as that feels to me, I like that, too. We're supposed to be hot for each other's bodies. Are you under the impression that I don't feel the same way?"

"You did say you wanted to wait. I, on the other hand, can't seem to wait another second."

"Because I want to get this relationship right, sweetheart. I want you to be happy, and you deserve a guy who doesn't fuck you before he dates you. And for the record, you make me crazy, too. The only thing that's kept me from trying desperately to get you naked is the fact that I want you to know that you're not just a hookup or a fling to me. That's the only thing that's kept me sane. That and the fact that I get myself off several times a day to stop myself from giving into temptation. When you put your hands on me, even that wasn't working. I had to get your hands off me before I completely forgot how badly I want to do everything right with you."

"You're doing everything right," I told him, a little gob smacked by his explanation. "*Nothing* you do with me is ever going to be wrong. I don't need you to officially date me, Devon. We've been going through the getting-to-know-you stuff for weeks now. And you have nothing to prove to me. I know that you care about me. It's obvious in everything you do for me."

"Fuck this shit then," he said gruffly as he snatched me out of the bed and carried me back toward his bedroom. "I'm going to show you exactly what it's like to be needy, horny, and out of control."

"We can wait," I said weakly. "I can keep on masturbating thinking about you for a little while longer. I want you to be happy, too."

"Fuck! Did you have to tell me that you're doing that?"

"You told me first," I said with a startled laugh.

He tossed me onto the bed, and the unbridled desire in his dark eyes made my breath catch.

God, he was beautiful when he looked like he was ready to snap.

He wasn't hiding how much he wanted me anymore, and it was one of the hottest things I'd ever seen.

He caught my gaze, and the need, hunger, and unbridled passion in his eyes made me feel like my heart was racing a thousand times a minute.

"I'll be happy when my cock is buried deep inside you and I'm finally able to put myself out of my misery," he said in a husky voice as he made short work of getting naked.

He kicked his sleep pants aside, and my eyes roamed over his muscular body lovingly, stopping at his gigantic and extremely hard cock.

"You're huge," I said before I could stop the words from leaving my lips.

I'd really only been with a couple of men in my life, and none of them had been built like Devon.

He shot me a cocky grin. "You look a little nervous. Where's my girl who couldn't wait for me to fuck her?"

"I still can't wait," I told him as I pulled my top over my head and tossed it on the floor. "But that's a little intimidating."

His expression sobered as he climbed on the bed and crawled toward me like a predator. "Condoms are in my bedside table."

I shook my head, "I'm on birth control, and I haven't been with anyone for a long time. I'm a women's health NP. I know I'm clean."

"I've never been with a woman without a condom, and I know I'm good, too," he said hoarsely. "How long has it been for you?"

"Years," I confessed. "I guess that's why I'm a little nervous."

"It's been a few years for me, too, Reese. I got sick of hookups. Don't be nervous. I'll figure out what your body is craving," he said as he pushed me back against the pillow and came down on top of me.

You!

All I wanted was Devon, and I didn't care what position that happened in as long as I could get him inside me as soon as possible.

I wrapped my arms around his neck and relaxed as he kissed me.

I savored the feeling of being skin-to-skin with him, and the sensation of falling into his embrace like I always did.

I'd fantasized about this so many times that it almost felt surreal to finally be this close to him.

This intimate.

This mesmerized.

When he finally released my mouth, he licked and nipped his way down the sensitive skin of my neck.

I balked a little when he stopped at my scar from the shooting and left a lingering kiss on the ugly mark.

"Everything about you is beautiful to me, Reese," he reminded me in a husky voice as he cupped my breasts.

I let out a huge sigh of happiness.

He wasn't being nice or trying to make me feel better.

Devon accepted me exactly as I was, and there was no better feeling in the world than that.

My back arched a little as he teased my nipples, tasting and nipping at each one of them until I was half crazy.

"Devon," I moaned, forgetting my nervousness.

Forgetting everything except the way he made me feel.

He moved oh-so-slowly down my belly and hooked his thumbs on my sleep shorts and lowered them down my legs.

When he tossed them aside and spread my legs, the anticipation of having him inside me was at a fevered pitch.

Except...he was in no rush to fuck me.

When I felt his warm breath on my pussy, another rush of heat flooded between my thighs.

"Fuck me, Devon," I pleaded.

"Not going to happen yet, sweetheart. I'm hungry and you're dinner right now. I've been wanting to do this for a very long time."

My experience with oral sex was almost nonexistent, and the short attempts in the past had been disappointing.

Devon teased, running his tongue over my inner thighs before he finally buried his face between them.

I sucked in a surprised breath as his hot mouth started to devour me like he really was a starving man.

The fact that he seemed to savor every moment of tasting me made the pleasure even more intense.

I let go and let myself get lost in sensation.

I speared my hands into his hair and held on for dear life.

He knew exactly how to use that wicked tongue and mouth to pleasure a woman, and when he slid a finger into my sheath and started fucking me with it, I released a throaty moan of ecstasy.

When he added a second finger, I nearly flew off the bed.

"Devon," I panted.

My body was wound tight, and I knew I was about to come.

My body craved release because the pleasure was almost too much to bear.

Like he could sense that I was on the edge, he focused on my clit, stimulating the tiny bundle of nerves until I flew over the edge.

I climaxed like I never had before, wave after wave hitting me until my entire body was shaking with my release.

My core finally unclenched from around Devon's fingers, but he didn't climb up my body immediately.

He seemed to want to savor every bit of the juices from my pussy before he finally made his way up my body.

My heart rate was starting to return to normal when his lips met mine.

I could taste myself on his lips, and it made me all the more eager to satisfy my man.

"Fuck me, Devon," I said as he released my lips. "I need you so much."

"It's going to be a short ride this time, sweetheart," he warned me. "I'm on the edge, and I've never been inside a female without a condom."

"I don't care," I told him in a desperate voice.

Devon didn't torture me by starting slow.

He buried himself to his balls inside me and stopped, giving me time to stretch and adjust.

"Oh, God," I cried out as my head fell back, relishing the feel of the two of us finally being this intimately connected.

I couldn't say that it was painful, but Devon stretched me to my limit. Even if it was painful, it would be worth it just to feel this way.

"Fuck!" Devon cursed. "You feel so damn good, Reese. This isn't going to last long."

I wrapped my legs around his waist, encouraging him to move. "Then fuck me hard and fast."

It didn't take any more encouragement for him to do just that.

And when he moved, I rose to meet every heart stopping thrust.

For a few moments, there was nothing but the sound of our harsh breaths and our bodies slapping together as Devon fucked me like a man possessed.

"Mine," he rasped near my ear. "You're finally fucking mine."

He punctuated each word with a powerful thrust that made me feel like he was claiming me.

It was so erotically possessive that I could feel my orgasm starting to unfurl in my belly.

I wanted to be taken and possessed by this man.

I wanted him to need me as much as I needed him.

Devon switched positions until every stroke of his cock stimulated my clit.

I moaned helplessly as I started to climax.

"That's it, Reese," he encouraged. "Come for me."

I exploded, my core strangling his cock.

My orgasm wasn't as intense as the last one, but it was just as satisfying.

Devon's release came seconds after mine, and I watched him as his large body tightened and he exploded deep in my womb.

He looked like he was out of control and primal, and it was one of the sexiest things I'd ever seen.

He wrapped his arms around my waist and rolled until I was on top of him.

Our bodies spent; we stayed locked together as we struggled to catch our breath.

When I could finally breathe again, he kissed me.

It was a kiss filled with devotion, tenderness, and adoration.

That was the exact moment when I realized that I didn't just care for this man.

I was falling head over heels in love with Devon Remington.

Chapter 21

Devon

"She didn't even look like the same woman to me," Kaleb said as we all sat in my family room after the women had left for Billings on Sunday.

We'd decided to get together after our women had abandoned us.

Tanner had dropped Hannah off to do her magic on Reese early this morning, and I was pretty sure that Kaleb had decided to come early with Anna to provide moral support.

Lauren had shown up here, too, rather than waiting to be picked up later.

Anna and Lauren really hadn't needed to be here that early, but the fact that they'd shown up for the entire transformation was a testament to how much they cared about Reese.

I had to admit that Reese had looked different when the women were done with her earlier this morning.

The red in her hair had been completely gone and replaced with a darker, muted shade of dark brown.

Her eye color had been changed to something less startling than her normal color, and Hannah had cut Reese's hair into a little shorter style.

Yeah, she might look different to most people, but she'd still looked like Reese to me.

And I still hated that she had decided to go to Billings in her current situation.

She was probably safe with her altered appearance, but I didn't like the thought of her being vulnerable. *At all.*

My protective instincts toward Reese had hit an all-time high since we'd gotten intimate on Friday.

The only thing we'd done yesterday that wasn't sexual was taking a ride during the afternoon.

Otherwise, we'd had sex in several areas of the house. I couldn't say we'd hit every room, but that was bound to happen sooner rather than later.

I couldn't be in the same vicinity as her and *not* want to touch her.

My dick was constantly hard whenever we were in the same room.

Not that I was complaining because Reese was always more than willing to take care of that problem.

We were starting to learn exactly how to make each other completely insane.

I'd always known how hot the chemistry was between the two of us, but with Reese, it was sex on a whole new level for me.

I always wanted to claim her body in a way that was probably a little twisted, but I didn't give a shit.

She was mine now, and there wasn't a damn thing in this world that was going to tear her away from me.

Except…maybe this trip to Billings.

Given the situation, it twisted my guts up to know that she was more exposed than she'd ever been since the shooting.

"They'll be fine, Devon," Tanner said gruffly. "If I thought they were in danger in any way, I would have insisted that Hannah stayed behind. There's no way anyone is going to recognize Reese as the same woman who had her photo in news articles.

"She needs to get out more for her mental health," Kaleb added. "This is a stressful situation that's gone on for too damn long. It's not healthy for her to feel this confined to a small town."

"Rationally, I know that," I said irritably. "I want Reese to have a little freedom to move, but that doesn't mean that I have to like it."

"We're always irrational when it comes to the safety of our women," Kaleb grumbled. "I worry about Anna constantly when I'm not able to travel with her. She's too vulnerable."

"And Hannah is pregnant, so I'm doubly protective," Tanner commented.

"I'm sorry for every time I gave you both a hard time about being overprotective," I said in a disgruntled voice.

Tanner grinned. "Now you know what it feels like to worry about someone who holds your happiness in their hands."

"It's pure hell," I admitted. "I don't know how you two have lived with it for longer than I have."

Tanner shrugged. "You learn to deal with it because any other choice is unthinkable. I'd rather worry than to not have Hannah in my life. I've been there, and I was a miserable asshole."

"I wish this whole thing was over. I wish they'd just apprehend the bastard," I told my brothers.

"It will get a little bit better if they do," Kaleb mused. "But those protective instincts are never going to go away completely. I think you're fucked, little brother. You better learn how to deal with it now."

I shot him an annoyed look. "Please don't tell me that I'm always going to feel this fucking crazy."

"Pretty much," Kaleb replied nonchalantly. "The protectiveness is part of who we are when we find a woman we can't and won't live without. You've obviously already made that choice regardless of your no commitment policy. You're committed to Reese."

"She's mine," I said testily. "Go ahead and say it. Everything is different now that I've found Reese. I know you're dying to make me eat my words."

I'd told them both that it was never going to happen to me because I'd never get into a relationship with any woman.

"We're not going to say that we told you so," Tanner assured me. "I think Kaleb and I both wanted you to find a woman who could stand up to your bullshit and knock you on your ass. But only because we wanted you to be happy. Neither one of us ever bought the crap that you were alone because you wanted to be. You just couldn't trust a female for some reason. Do you want to share that reason with us now?"

"Not really," I answered. "But I will."

Kaleb and Tanner looked surprised that I was finally willing to share something I'd been quiet about for years.

I'd hidden the truth from my brothers long enough, and after telling Reese about what had happened, it didn't seem that difficult to share it with my brothers.

I went through the whole story again with my two siblings.

"Fucking hell!" Kaleb cursed. "Why didn't you tell us? You could have died, Devon."

"I didn't die," I said, pointing out that obvious fact. "Both of you had your shit together back then. You were already in New York and busting your asses to be successful. I felt like an idiot, like the failure little brother who couldn't get things right. I looked up to both of you. I didn't really want to admit that I'd fallen for some ridiculous bullshit while you two were responsible adults trying to start a company for all of us."

"You were young," Tanner argued. "You weren't even quite out of college yet, and you were never a failure. You graduated with high honors for fuck's sake. We were proud of you. You're allowed a few dumb mistakes, Devon. Kaleb and I have made plenty of them. We would have been pissed as hell because of what happened, but you should have called us when you were injured. I get not wanting to call our parents because they would have flipped out, but we would have been there for you."

"I know that," I said ruefully. "But it wasn't something I wanted to discuss with anyone until now. I just wanted to put it behind me and move on."

"Reese changed all that," Kaleb guessed.

"I had to tell her," I told him truthfully. "I didn't want her to think that I didn't take our relationship seriously. I had a reputation as a hookup guy who never made a commitment. She needed to know why."

Kaleb nodded. "I agree. I'm glad you finally decided to share it with us, too. Your whole attitude never made sense to me. Now it does. You finally found the woman you could trust enough to take a leap of faith."

"I had to take that leap or let her go," I said truthfully. "Reese could have never been a fling for me. She probably deserves a man much better than me, but I'll figure out how to be a good boyfriend. I just don't have much practice."

"You don't need it," Kaleb informed me. "You already make her feel special every day because you put her needs before your own. You're proving that right now. You kept your mouth shut about her going to Billings this morning even though I knew it was eating your guts out to let her go."

"Did I really have a choice?" I asked drily. "Reese is her own woman. She was going to go."

She'd already warned me about that, and I'd had to accept her decision.

"Maybe not," Tanner considered. "But you could have been an asshole about it."

"I couldn't," I told him. "She was too damn excited about the whole thing. For once in my life, it was impossible for me to be an asshole and spoil this for her." I paused before I asked both of my brothers, "How else can I be the guy she needs? I've thought about dozens of things I could give her, but she doesn't really care about my money or the material things I can give her."

"Hannah and Anna don't care about the material things, either," Tanner told me. "Hannah has always had her own ambitions, even after I became wealthy enough to support both of us. Support Reese in hers. Don't make the mistakes that I did. Her career is just as important as yours, even though you're a billionaire."

"Reese does something more important than I do," I answered. "She saves lives and takes care of people. I just make a lot of money. Don't get me wrong, I care about Remington as much as you two, and

I wouldn't want to do anything else, but Reese's work is important. Anything that's important to her is important to me. I watched and learned from your mistakes with Hannah."

"That's probably the one good thing about being the youngest," Kaleb joked. "You can learn from the stupid mistakes we made and not make the same ones."

I grinned at him. "It's definitely a benefit. But it wasn't always easy being the tag along little brother when we were younger."

There wasn't much of an age difference between the three of us, but I'd always felt like the one who was lagging behind sometimes.

"You weren't that big of a pain in the ass," Tanner drawled. "But I'm damn glad you're with Reese now. What's the future plan?"

I shook my head. "We haven't looked that far ahead. I try not to go there and just appreciate the fact that she's in my life and that she wants my sorry ass. I don't want to scare her off by wanting to plan our entire future, but it's not easy for me *not* to talk about it."

"That's probably a good idea given the situation right now," Kaleb said. "I went through something similar with Anna. Her life was in Los Angeles. Mine was here. I would have relocated for her, but I'm damn glad that she liked it here and wanted to stay. If she'd wanted to keep doing big tours, I would have found a way to deal with that, too. I want to protect her, but I don't want to stifle her career. She's busted her ass and sacrificed a lot for her music career."

"It's going to be a little bit different for you," Tanner warned. "Hannah grew up here and her mom is here. Anna didn't have family in California. Reese's parents are in Spokane, and from what I've heard, they're pretty close."

"I'm not even sure she'd be willing to relocate because of that," I grumbled. "She's an only child. Her parents are past retirement age, but they work because they still can, and they want to do it. She's going to want to be close to them as they get older."

"Can't say that I blame her," Tanner answered. "I know how important it is for us to be close to Mom so we can support her."

"Don't put those roadblocks in your way right now, Devon," Kaleb warned. "If you love each other, everything can be worked out.

Spokane isn't that far away. You do have a private jet. I know the need to figure out your future is pretty strong, but sometimes you have to take things one step at a time."

Love?

It suddenly hit me that I actually *was* romantically in love for the first damn time in my life.

Why was I only figuring this out now?

Maybe because it had started with friendship.

Followed by fondness and physical attraction.

And then it had morphed into this monstrous obsession that I couldn't quite get a grip on, no matter how hard I tried to contain it.

I couldn't say that it was love at first sight for me.

Then again, I was probably slow when it came to matters of the heart since I'd never found a woman I'd felt this way about before.

Love?

Fuck! I had no idea if Reese felt the same way. We were only officially dating right now.

I knew that she cared about me, but love was completely different.

I was going to have to be a damn good boyfriend to make her fall in love with me or I was going to be completely screwed.

Chapter 22

Reese

"Devon Remington," I said in an exasperated voice the following Saturday as we relaxed in the hot tub after our workout and swim. "If you don't stop buying me things, I'm going to run out of space to put those things in this house."

Every single day, he'd brought home more things for me, and every single day, those gifts became a little more outrageous.

Jewelry. Very *expensive* jewelry that he thought a guy should give to his woman.

Expensive cooking items I'd mentioned at one time or another during our relationship.

A whole new wardrobe that had filled the entire second walk-in in his master bedroom because he'd heard me say weeks ago that I hadn't brought a lot of clothing with me to Crystal Fork. That wardrobe hadn't left out a single item of clothing, and all of those items were very pricey designer brands. He'd given me the option of returning any of the things I didn't like for something else, but surprisingly, everything he'd chosen was something I would have

B. A. Scott

bought myself if I was the type of woman who spent that much on clothing.

I'd gotten electronics.

He'd purchased every scent available of the fragrance mists that I loved, and they had *a lot* of scents.

Last night, he'd brought home a mountain bike because I'd mentioned that trying the sport with Hannah might be fun.

A few moments ago, he'd asked me what my dream car was, but I'd put a stop to that purchase by telling him I'd have to kill him if he bought me a new vehicle.

His thoughtfulness was overwhelmingly sweet, but it was getting to be absolute lunacy.

Surely no woman expected all of that, not even from a billionaire boyfriend.

I'd tried to put my foot down before, but he'd just kept on giving me more gifts.

Now, enough was enough.

He *had* to stop.

He grinned at me. "Impossible. This is a very large home."

"Devon," I said as I shot him a warning look. "You've given me a lifetime worth of gifts in a matter of days."

"You're worth a hell of a lot more than a few gifts," he said crankily.

My heart melted.

I loved his thoughtfulness and his generous nature, but the gifts had to stop. It was way too much for any woman to handle. Especially one who didn't remember getting very many gifts from past boyfriends.

I hadn't fallen for him because he was a wealthy billionaire.

I had fallen for him because he was an incredible guy.

I moved closer to him and wrapped my arms around his neck. "I don't need gifts. I already have what I want. I have you."

His arms wrapped around my waist tightly and possessively.

"That doesn't sound like a great deal to me," he said drily. "I think gifts are definitely necessary."

Most of the time, Devon didn't seem to recognize just how important he was in my life, or how much he'd already done for me just by being supportive.

Spending the day with the girls in Billings last Sunday had been one of the most freeing experiences I'd had in a long time.

It had felt so good just to do normal things with my friends for the day.

To feel normal again meant everything to me.

I know that it had killed Devon not to protest, but he hadn't said a word that morning as Hannah was altering my appearance or when we'd left.

He'd simply kissed me and told me to have fun and to be careful.

We'd definitely had fun, and I hadn't needed to be that careful because I knew I looked different enough to fool anyone who wasn't close to me.

We'd done the massages, had a picnic lunch in the park, shopped like crazy, and had stopped on the way home for cookies, which Devon had highly appreciated and devoured within a day.

He treated all of my fears like they were perfectly normal given my circumstances and history, and he listened to me, even when he didn't have all of the answers.

Just having this man in my life was a miracle to me, and I didn't need any of the gifts he insisted on giving me.

However, I didn't want to hurt him, either, by flatly refusing something he'd gone to the trouble to get me, but I was at the point where I just couldn't handle another gift.

He'd already given me so much even before he'd started buying me the material things.

Devon was also a very unselfish lover who made my pleasure his priority.

I insisted on doing the same, but he usually didn't want to find his release when I gave him oral sex.

He always told me that he'd rather get off deep inside of *me*.

I had to say that the man had been right about multiple orgasm. Turns out that I was capable of having them with a man like him.

I was still discovering parts of my sexuality that I'd never known had existed before him.

"Have I ever told you how lucky I feel that you're my guy?" I asked as I straddled him and nuzzled my face into his neck. "Not because of the material things you give me but because you treat me with the respect a partner deserves."

"I doubt you felt that way when I was bossing you around in bed last night," he said hoarsely.

Now *that* had been incredibly hot for me. "It was pretty sexy," I told him playfully. "You can boss me around in bed any time you want."

I'd quickly discovered that Devon sometimes wanted to be in complete control in the bedroom, and I was all for that.

The bossy, demanding side of him did it for me sexually.

We were currently naked in the hot tub, and he squeezed my ass approvingly.

Because I was literally on top of him, I could feel that he was impossibly hard even though we'd just had wild sex as part of our workout.

It felt like we could never get enough of each other.

I'd thought that we'd cool off somewhat after the initial lust had calmed down a little.

I'd thought wrong.

The more we'd gotten to know each other's bodies, the hotter that part of our relationship had become.

I was impossibly addicted to being this intimate and this close to Devon.

He grasped a lock of my hair and pulled my head back so he could see my face.

Our eyes met, and heat rushed between my thighs as I saw the hungry look in his eyes.

My heart stuttered because I'd probably never get used to the way he looked at me like I was the only woman in the world that he'd ever wanted.

"Devon," I said weakly. "We need to talk about this gift giving thing. It's out of control."

He put his hand on the nape of my neck, and without a word, he pulled my lips to his.

He'd ignored my comment, but as soon as the erotic embrace began, all thoughts about the gifts flew out of my head.

Devon consumed me, and I didn't give a shit about anything else on the planet.

He slipped his hand between the two of us, and he caressed my clit while he devoured my mouth.

Once my brain was completely muddled by his possessive kiss, he released my lips and put his mouth on my breasts.

I'd completely forgotten about how much I hated the scar on my chest because Devon seemed to enjoy tormenting my breasts—scar, or no scar.

In moments, he had me moaning and moving my hips against his fingers, silently pleading for release.

"Fuck this!" Devon growled as he picked me up and laid me down on a plush rug next to the tub. "It's too damn hot in here, and having sex in a hot tub is overrated."

I smiled as he got out of the spa with an impatient, wild look in his eyes.

He was next to me in a heartbeat, taking up where he'd left off in the hot tub.

He kissed me again and his fingers resumed their previous activity of making me crazy.

A fresh rush of juices flooded my pussy. "Devon," I crooned when he finally released my lips, my body tight with need.

"I want you hot and wet when you take my cock," he rasped against my ear.

He thrust his fingers into my sheath as though he was testing whether or not I was wet enough for his liking.

"I'm ready," I said insistently. "I need you inside me."

I didn't want or need any more foreplay or teasing.

I just wanted…him.

He moved to his back and pulled me on top of him. "Then ride me," he demanded. "Show me exactly what you want."

B. A. Scott

I didn't hesitate. I grasped his enormous, hard cock and slowly lowered myself down until the entire length of him was embedded inside me.

I let out a huge sigh as he stretched me to my limits.

He went deep this way, but there was only a stretching sensation while my body accepted him.

"Fuck!" he cursed in a sexy, husky voice as he grasped my ass. "Do you have any idea what it's like for me to watch you do that? You're the sexiest woman I've ever laid eyes on."

I actually felt sexy.

I felt alive.

I felt…adored.

"Take what you need, Reese," he commanded.

I ground my hips down, trying to get impossibly deeper and to give my clit the pressure it was begging for right now.

Then I lifted and sank down again.

Devon grasped my ass a little harder, and I could tell he was forcing himself not to take control.

He was letting me set the pace.

Letting me satisfy myself.

This wasn't a position we'd done a lot because I wasn't used to it, but he was obviously determined to make me love it.

I put my hands on his broad shoulders and watched his face as I sped up the pace.

His eyes darkened, and I could tell that he liked it, so I kept moving faster.

"Christ!" he cursed as his hands moved to my hips and started to guide me. "You make me completely insane."

I sat up as he pulled me up and down, his hips rising to meet every thrust.

I savored it when Devon lost control.

I marveled that I could actually make that happen.

"Touch those gorgeous tits," he insisted. "Feel every bit of pleasure you can get. Be greedy. Your pussy strangling my cock feels so fucking good that I'm not going to last long."

I'd never done *that* before, but nothing I ever did with Devon felt wrong to me.

I cupped my breast and pinched my nipples. The sensation went straight to the place that the two of us were joined.

It was such a pleasurable sensation that I did it over and over again as Devon thrust his hips up to keep slamming inside of me.

"Devon," I cried out as I threw my head back and let out a very loud and uncontrolled moan.

I could feel my climax rising up to meet me, and when Devon moved one of his hands to stimulate my clit, I imploded.

"That's it, baby," he said harshly. "Milk my cock."

I didn't have any choice in the matter. My climax was fierce, and my core clenched around his massive cock in powerful spasms.

He found his own release with a groan that sounded like a combination of intense pleasure and relief.

I leaned down and kissed him, an embrace that was both sensual and soothing.

I had to bite my lip to keep from telling him how much I loved him.

How much he'd changed my entire life just by being in it.

Those words had almost tumbled from my lips spontaneously because I'd desperately needed to say them.

My heart ached to let those emotions out, but it was probably too soon to be talking about love.

I knew exactly how I felt, but I'd be crushed if he didn't or couldn't say those words to me.

I can wait.

I'd waited thirty-two years to find a man like Devon. I could force myself not to say those words and screw up what we had at the moment.

He held me tight as I buried my face in his neck and caught my breath.

I had him.

He was my guy.

We had right now.

We were crazy about each other.

For now, that would have to be enough.

Chapter 23

Devon

"Where's Reese?" I asked my mother as I entered her kitchen the next day.

We were having a family dinner tonight at my mother's place, and Reese had come over early to help Mom.

Since they were going to be cooking, I'd stayed behind for a while to work on a song that I was co-writing with Anna.

Reese had subtly hinted that she wouldn't mind having some girl time with my mom, and I certainly wouldn't be helping them cook dinner.

Reese was slowly starting to learn to manage her PTSD with the help of her new counselor, and I was fairly sure it helped her to talk to my mother, too.

The two of them had gotten even tighter since the truth about Reese's past had been revealed.

Mom looked from the food she was stirring in a big pot and smiled at me. "Reese and I went for a walk earlier to see the progress on Cole and Asher's land. We sat for a while at the property border by that big Ponderosa Pine. I think I left my phone there. She offered to get it while I watched our dinner. You just missed her, but it shouldn't take her long."

I'd lightened up a little about Reese being alone while she was in Crystal Fork.

I still didn't let her ride alone because the trails were pretty remote, but she should be safe enough going to the Ponderosa Pine and back. It wasn't like that big pine tree was miles deep into Mom's property.

"We're all in the dining room," Kaleb said as he strolled into the kitchen. "So what's the latest news about Cole and Asher?"

Cole and Asher Remington were our cousins.

They'd left Crystal Fork years ago and had never really stayed in touch.

I'd connected a few times with Cole in the last few months because they were building homes on our uncle's old property and planning on moving home now that they'd sold their multi-billion-dollar tech company in Austin.

Asher was a mystery to me.

My communication had been sparse with Cole, but at least he'd been cordial.

Asher had never bothered to answer anyone in the family when they'd tried to contact him.

Since their father had been an asshole and an alcoholic, we'd never really mingled with our cousins much when we were younger.

My father had been estranged from his brother, and my cousins hadn't seemed to want to have much to do with us, either.

Cole and Asher had always had a hard edge to them and were pretty anti-social. As far as I knew, they hadn't changed much.

Looking back on that as an adult, I was pretty sure their behavior had a lot to do with their father.

I suspected he was an abusive dick.

I wasn't quite sure how they were going to be accepted back into Crystal Fork.

A lot of the townspeople still believed that they'd murdered their own father, but I'd never really believed it was true. Unfortunately,

I had no real proof that they hadn't done it because the murder had never been solved.

That property next to Mom's had been abandoned for a long time, and in my mind, it was past time that it was occupied again.

"We could really only see Cole's home," Mom said. "Asher built his on the other side of the property. Cole's home is lovely though. I'm glad that they're both coming home. That property is their birthright."

"I doubt they care," I said drily. "They're both filthy rich."

"They're Remingtons," my mother insisted. "Montana is in their blood."

"Cole said they're going to breed horses," I informed them. "And they have a bunch of other business interests around the world. Their tech company just happened to be their biggest one."

"I hope they've gotten a little friendlier," Kaleb said wryly. "I've reached out to Asher, but he never returned my calls."

"Don't count on it," I warned. "I have a feeling they're coming back to figure out who killed their father. I'm not sure why they care because they weren't convicted of the crime, and I'm not sure they even liked the asshole."

"Devon," my mother said in a scolding voice.

I held up a hand. "Okay, I'm sorry for cursing, but you know it's true."

My mother shook her head. "I'm going to welcome them with open arms. They are my nephews. Your father felt horrible because there was nothing he could do for them, but they swore they weren't being neglected. There wasn't much he could do. I think he'd want me to welcome them back as adults. He'd be happy they were back. He'd want them to be part of our family."

"Just don't get your hopes up," Kaleb warned. "They may not want to be part of the family."

"Well, I'll still defend them," Mom said stubbornly. "I never thought they killed your uncle, and I don't believe it now. I don't think it's fair that people call them the black-sheep Remingtons. It bothers me. Those two boys did nothing wrong."

Kaleb rubbed a hand over his face. "I don't think any of us believe that they killed our uncle, but it's going to be hard for them to prove who did after all these years. If they couldn't solve the crime years ago, I doubt it's going to be solved now."

"Did Cole say when they're making their move?" my mother asked.

"He never really said," I admitted. "He's not the kind of guy who overshares anything or explains anything he does, but I'm thinking it will be before winter."

"Everything looks ready there," Mom said excitedly. "Even the barns."

Kaleb shot me a concerned look, and I understood exactly why he was worried.

Mom did have her hopes up that we'd all become one big, happy, Remington family someday, but that was highly unlikely.

It was going to be heartbreaking for her when she realized that our cousins didn't give a damn about being family.

Cole was cordial at best, and I was pretty sure that Asher held more than a little animosity toward the rest of the family.

Both of them were known to be ice-cold, both in their business dealings and in their personal lives.

Cole might be distant and cool with my mother, but I doubted he'd outright snub her.

Asher had a reputation for being an ornery and unpleasant guy, and I doubted that he'd feel the least bit remorseful about blowing my mother off and hurting her feelings.

Neither one of them were going to be neighborly, and that would end up pissing off both myself and my brothers.

Mom had been through a lot with the loss of my dad, and she was getting older.

We were all protective of her, and it would be trouble if they hurt her in any way.

That's why I'd tried to reach out to Cole more.

I'd wanted to see for myself if he was as big of an asshole as he was rumored to be.

Unfortunately, he was pretty unreadable and distant, so I couldn't be sure if the rumors about him were true.

Hell, people thought my brothers and I were sharks.

We were when it came to business.

But we gave a damn about our family.

My mother moved to the fridge, and I leaned closer to Kaleb.

"If they hurt her, I'll hurt both of them," I said to Kaleb in a low voice that my mother couldn't hear.

He nodded. "We all will."

"Is there anything I can do to help," Hannah asked as she waddled into the kitchen.

She was getting close to her due date, and she was starting to look a little uncomfortable.

"You can go into the living room and put your feet up," Mom scolded. "Your feet have been swelling lately."

"The doctor said I'm fine," Hannah argued.

"She's right," Tanner said as he entered behind her with Anna directly behind him.

I watched as Tanner put his arm around Hannah and a protective hand on his wife's abdomen.

Tanner probably had the calmest demeanor of all of us brothers, but he was looking a little frazzled lately.

He was obviously worried about his wife and her upcoming delivery.

I couldn't blame him.

It had to be hell to know that your wife was about to go through a lot of pain to bring your kid into the world.

"Where's Reese?" Lauren asked as she walked into the room.

My mother explained to her that she'd lost her phone, and that Reese had gone to retrieve it.

I glanced up at the kitchen clock.

It had been a while since she'd left.

The pine tree was a short hike, but she should be getting back by now. She was a fast walker, and she'd be hurrying in case Mom needed her help.

"Maybe I should go meet her," I said out loud.

Kaleb slapped me on the back. "Relax. She hasn't been gone that long, and I don't think anything is going to happen to her here."

I pulled my phone from the pocket of my jeans and sent her a short text, simply asking if she was getting close to the house.

Reese was always good about answering my texts quickly because she knew I would be worried if she didn't.

Everyone around me looked at me like I was being a little over-protective, but I didn't give a shit.

There was someone out there in the world who wanted the woman I loved dead, and that made me slightly edgy almost all of the time.

Ralph had told me a few days ago that it had been a while since they'd gotten a location on Kline.

It had also been weeks since he'd sent a threatening message to Reese on her old digital devices.

He'd also said that he wondered if Burke Kline had decided to commit suicide and was dead somewhere and no one had found him yet.

In my mind, that asshole offing himself would be the best-case scenario, but I wished someone would find his dead body so this could be over for Reese.

My family kept chatting as a minute ticked by.

And then two.

And then three.

By minute five, something in my gut was telling me something wasn't right.

"Maybe she hasn't seen it," Kaleb suggested.

"She'd hear it," I told him gruffly. "It's not exactly noisy out there. Something's wrong. I can feel it. I'm going out into the fields."

"I'm coming with you," Kaleb said immediately. "Tanner, take care of your wife, and call Ralph and tell him we might need him out here. It might be a false alarm, but I'd rather be safe than sorry. We're going to find Reese."

"I'll call him on our way," Tanner answered as he fell into step behind us after shooting a glance at my mother.

Mom nodded, silently agreeing to watch over Hannah while he was gone.

Kaleb had enough sense to grab my dad's shotgun from the front closet before we were all out the door.

Chapter 24

Reese

"Would you care to explain to me exactly why that lunatic hates you?" the man next to me asked in a dry voice.

My entire body was shaking with fear.

The two of us were tied by the ankles and wrists, and then we'd been roped together so it was impossible for us to get to our feet.

Somehow, Burke Kline had found me, and he was even crazier than he'd been when he'd shot Kyle and I in Spokane.

The only thing that had stopped him from killing me almost immediately after he'd snuck up on me at the pine tree had been Cole Remington.

Cole had been in his barns, and he'd heard Burke ranting and probably saw him punching me in the face as he'd stepped back outside again.

Unfortunately, he hadn't seen the gun that Burke had been holding until he'd sprinted over to us, and it was too late.

Burke had been ready to put a bullet in my head when Cole had distracted him enough to make Burke hesitate.

Cole had told him that he was filthy rich and could give him the funds and the tools to make an escape, but that he wasn't going to shoot me out in the open where anyone could hear and see it happen.

Technically, we hadn't been on his property, but Burke hadn't known that.

In the end, both Cole and I had been taken prisoner by Burke and were tied together in the downstairs level of Cole's new home.

Cole had told Burke to go help himself to some food that was in the refrigerator, and we'd been tied up and left here while Burke was stuffing his face upstairs.

At this point, I wasn't sure if Cole was just as evil as Burke, or if he was trying to save my life.

Maybe I was an idiot, but it was hard for me to believe that someone who had so many of Devon's facial features was that evil. Cole looked like a Remington. The resemblance wasn't as pronounced as it was between the three Remington brothers, but he definitely looked like family.

Since I wasn't dead yet, I quickly and briefly explained what had happened in Spokane.

I also told him that I was being hidden in Crystal Fork until Burke was apprehended.

"He's going to kill you, too," I said in a tremulous voice. "He's insane, and he won't leave any witnesses, even if you do give him what he wants."

"I have no intention of giving him what he wants," Cole informed me. "If he would have taken that gun off you for even a single second, this would already be over, and that bastard would be dead. So, you're Devon's woman?"

I'd briefly mentioned that Devon and I were together in my explanation, so I simply said, "Yes. My name is Reese."

He'd already told Burke that his name was Cole but hadn't mentioned that he was a Remington.

But that was something I already knew.

Billionaire Undeceived

"I guarantee that my cousin is already looking for you. He's a hardheaded Remington," Cole said calmly. "But I'm not counting on him finding us before this idiot puts a bullet in our heads."

"You're probably right," I said shakily. "I should have been back to Millie's place by now, but I don't think he's going to be looking for me in your house. Does he know you're here?"

"No," Cole said abruptly. "I don't make it a habit to explain my whereabouts to anyone. I only planned on being here for a few days. I wanted to check the construction work that was done here. Luckily, I stocked a few days of food in the refrigerator. He'll be eating for a while. He looks like he hasn't had food in a long time. But you're going to be ready to run when I tell you to run. Don't look back. Just haul ass and get out the door."

"I can't exactly run like this," I answered nervously.

"I'm good with ropes and knots," he said simply. "Neither one of us are going to die here at the hands of this asshole."

"You weren't going to let him shoot me and try to save yourself with money and supplies, were you?" I wasn't sure how I knew that, but I knew it was true.

"I like my new home, and I don't want blood on the carpet before I can even move in," he said stoically. "This area is probably going to be a man cave. It would be damn hard to enjoy a football game on a big screen knowing a woman had been murdered in the room."

I probably would have laughed at his black sense of humor if I wasn't completely terrified.

This man might be gruff and a little humorless, but he was no murderer like some people thought.

He *was* trying to save my life.

Devon hadn't talked much about his cousins, but he had told me that they'd never been close and that they were moving back to Crystal Fork.

Millie had told me more about Cole and Asher's background and what had happened to force them away from Crystal Fork.

167

"Why didn't you just ignore what Burke was doing to me?" I asked him, trying to distract myself from the thought of Burke shooting me...again.

"I don't get into people's business," Cole said roughly. "But no man should ever lay a hand on a woman or a child."

I could feel the ropes binding us together start to loosen.

Obviously, he hadn't been lying when he'd said he was good with rope and knots. "What's the plan?"

Burke had taken our cell phones, including Millie's that I'd just retrieved before he'd found me. So there was no way we could call for help even if Cole could get us free.

I was still trembling, but I was trained to keep my head together in stressful situations.

I needed to think and keep my wits about me.

I felt the same way as Cole did.

I didn't want to give Burke the satisfaction of dying here today.

"I figure we have at least another fifteen minutes before he comes back down to kill us both. I stocked plenty of beer in the fridge along with the food, so he'll knock down at least a few of them before he comes back. We need to get the fuck out of here. It's going to be risky because we'll have to pass the kitchen to get out the door. You're a small woman and I'm a big guy. Stay close to me and out of his line of fire. You got that?"

Maybe some people would cringe and not ask questions when this man gave an order, but I wasn't most people.

"But that would put you in his line of fire," I argued.

"Better me than you," he quipped. "My cousin would kill me anyway if I let anything happen to you."

The ropes around us gave way, and Cole quickly used his bound hands to untie my feet and hands so I could untie his.

He shoved all the ropes aside impatiently and grabbed my hand to pull me to my feet.

I stumbled a little as the circulation started to return to my extremities.

"You okay?" he asked in a no-nonsense baritone.

"Yeah," I lied as I rubbed my hands together to hurry the process.

My circulation would come back, and I had no desire to complain. I didn't want to stay here any longer than Cole did.

I desperately hoped that Burke's back was turned so he couldn't see us escaping.

If something happened to Cole while he was trying to save my life, I wasn't sure I could live with myself.

He was an innocent bystander.

I was the woman that Burke desperately wanted to kill.

I didn't like the fact that he planned to shield my body with his, but he'd made it clear that this wasn't happening any other way.

It was a risk, but if we didn't do something, we'd both end up dead for certain.

"Remember what I said," he said in a warning voice.

"Please don't get shot," I said in a tearful voice.

A small, cocky smirk formed on his lips. "That's not part of the plan."

He put me behind him as he climbed the stairs and placed my hand on his belt so that he knew that I was right behind him.

For a man as large as Cole, he managed to move stealthily up the steps.

My heart was beating so hard and fast that I was almost afraid that Burke would actually hear it.

I took a deep breath and silently let it out.

Don't panic, Reese. Not now. You know what you have to do. Run fast if Burke spots you, and make sure that Cole is right there close to you.

When we reached the top of the stairs, Cole switched positions, put his arm around me and kept me shielded from the kitchen.

We moved soundlessly.

The very brief glimpse I got of the kitchen before Cole blocked my view told me that Burke didn't have his back to us, but his attention was on his food and beer.

We'd almost passed the kitchen when Cole shouted, "Run Reese! Now."

I instantly knew that Burke had seen us when he called out, "Stop! You aren't getting away from me this time, bitch!"

I ran, with Cole right behind me, still shielding me from Burke.

I almost froze in place as we ran out the door and a gunshot exploded behind us, but Cole kept pushing me onward until we were down the steps.

Everything happened so quickly after that gunshot that I was confused.

Another gunshot exploded.

I was suddenly tackled and taken to the ground with an exceptionally large, heavy body on top of me.

I'd started to scream before Devon rasped into my ear, "It's me, Reese. It's me. Are you hurt?"

I stopped screaming the moment I heard his voice.

Devon was on top of me, trying to protect me.

"No," I said in a panicked voice that didn't sound like my own.

"He's dead," I heard Ralph say from a short distance away.

"Cole!" I gasped, terrified.

"I'm still alive," Cole said in a deep voice from right beside me.

I struggled to get free, and Devon finally rose from his protective position on top of me.

"W-what just happened," I said, my brain still not comprehending what had just taken place.

"Kline is dead," Devon said as he wrapped his arms around me. "Ralph shot him."

"Cole?" I asked as I turned in Devon's arms to see Cole laying on the ground beside me.

I scrambled over to Cole when I saw a pool of blood that was seeping from a wound on his side. "He's hurt," I said as tears filled my eyes.

"Getting shot wasn't part of the plan, but I don't think I'm going to die from it," Cole said weakly.

I lifted his shirt. "Somebody get me some towels or something to put pressure on the wound. Talk to me, Cole."

Devon immediately removed his shirt and handed it to me to use to stop the bleeding.

"The helicopter is coming," Kaleb said. "We can get him to Billings faster that way. You can ride with him, Reese."

"I'm going to live, Reese," Cole assured me. "But I'm pretty pissed that I'm going to end up with blood on my new porch."

Those were the last words I heard from Cole before he promptly passed out.

Chapter 25

Devon

"I'm going to owe you for this for the rest of my life," I told Cole solemnly as I sat in a chair next to his bedside in the hospital.

They were keeping my cousin overnight. He'd lost quite a bit of blood, and he'd be getting more fluids and antibiotics before they discharged him tomorrow.

He'd gotten damn lucky. Kline had shot him with a small caliber weapon, and the location where he'd been grazed had been extremely fortunate. There were no injuries to any major organs or bone.

The bullet hadn't entered his body, but it had left a nasty gash in his side that had bled like crazy and had needed quite a few sutures to repair.

It had taken me a while to figure out exactly what had occurred. I hadn't learned everything until I'd gotten most of it from Reese.

I was still fucking livid that Kline had punched her hard enough to leave her face black and blue, but the doctor had assured me that she'd be fine as soon as the bruises healed.

She'd been discharged and I asked my family to take care of her until I could get home.

Knowing my cousin had saved Reese's life had left me feeling like I owed it to him to be here.

"You don't owe me shit," he rumbled. "I did what any guy would have done if he saw some asshole pounding on a woman."

He'd done more than that, and I knew it. Reese had given me the details. Cole had shielded Reese, knowing full well that he could end up shot because of it.

Even after he'd taken that gunshot, he'd still kept Reese moving so he could get her out of danger.

He could have walked away from the whole situation and just called the police, but he hadn't.

"If you ever need a favor, I'm there for it," I said. "If you ever need family, I'm there for that, too."

"You must have it bad for Reese if you're going that far," Cole said drily.

"I love her," I said honestly. "When you saved her life, you saved mine, too."

Cole was quiet for a moment before he answered, "For what it's worth, she seems like a pretty incredible woman. She was pretty brave and calm about the whole thing, even though I could tell that she was terrified."

"She is incredible," I verified. "Her entire world was turned upside down a year ago when she was shot, and her friend and colleague was killed. She left everything that was important to her and has been living under an assumed identity ever since. It's taken a toll on her, but it's hasn't broken her."

My phone pinged, and I pulled it out of my pocket, not surprised to see that the text was from Reese.

"It's Reese," I told Cole. "She's worried about you and wants to know if you're okay. She wants to know what treatment you're getting. She's a nurse practitioner."

Cole smirked. "I have to say that I've never had a woman worry about me before."

I shrugged. "It's who she is. She worries about everyone but herself."

"Tell her I'm going home tomorrow and that I'm fine," he suggested. "Let her know you'll be home soon. The nurse is going to give me some pain drugs, and that will knock me out. You don't need to stay here and babysit me."

I typed a message back to Reese and put my phone back into my pocket as I said, "You're my family, Cole. I'm not here to babysit you."

"Go home to your woman, Devon," Cole replied. "She needs you more than I do."

After this man had literally taken a bullet for Reese and stopped Kline from killing her more than once, he was always going to be family to me. Whether he wanted family or not.

I wished I had been there for Reese myself, but we'd still been searching the grounds near Cole's house when he and Reese had flown out the front door.

I hadn't known that Kline had found her, and I didn't know that Cole was here.

During Kline's rant and assault of Reese, he'd mentioned that he'd finally decided to follow her lead detective from Spokane to try to get information about where she was hiding.

Although Reese was under an assumed identity, Ralph was not.

The timing couldn't have been worse.

My mother's place was on the way into town from the highway.

Kline had just happened to see Reese as she was walking through the field closer to the road.

The bastard had stalked her to the property border before he'd snatched her.

"I'm so fucking glad that asshole is dead," I said, hating that one moment of vulnerability had led to Reese being found.

Ralph had shot Kline just in time.

If he hadn't, the bastard would have gotten another shot off from the porch that could have killed Reese or Cole.

"I'm with you on that," Cole answered. "If I'd gotten a single second of opportunity, he would have been dead. But he never took the gun off Reese. He made her restrain my hands and legs before he tied her up. I couldn't risk her getting shot if I jumped him."

"Reese said you could have just called the police and not gotten involved," I mused.

He shot me a disbelieving look. "I might be an asshole, but I wasn't going to watch some lunatic beating on a female. I didn't know she was your woman at the time, but that shit is never going to fly with me. There are certain times when I don't mind getting my hands dirty. That's one of the few things that sets me off."

I was damn glad that Cole had a few triggers.

He'd always been pretty cool and distant when we'd spoken before, but there was obviously still a decent human inside Cole's body. The decent side was apparently just harder to find in my cousin than it was in most people.

"You here for good now?" I questioned him.

He shook his head. "I was just here for a few days to do a final inspection of the work on the houses and the horse facilities. I didn't plan to get shot."

"Did you call Asher?"

"Nah," he said nonchalantly. "He'd lose his shit, even though it's just a flesh wound, and he's out of the country on business. There's nothing he can do. I'll be out of the hospital tomorrow. My jet is at the airport. I'll probably fly home sooner than I'd planned."

I shook my head. "Not happening. I'll be here tomorrow to pick you up. Everybody is going to want to see you, especially my mother. You have family here to take care of you. Be nice to Mom. She cares about you and Asher. She's excited that you're both coming home."

He shrugged. "I have no reason not to be nice to her. I don't have any hard feelings toward Millie."

"Well, that's good to hear," my mother's voice said cheerfully from the doorway. "Because I'm here, and I'm going to make sure that you get well. Go home, Devon. I'll take over from here. I've already talked to the nurse about making that comfortable recliner into my bed for the night."

I rose from that comfortable recliner and kissed my mother's cheek.

I smirked at Cole as his brows rose and he said, "That's not necessary."

He obviously didn't know my mother well.

I'd already known that she'd be back as soon as everyone was settled in at home.

"It is necessary," Mom said as she sat the bag of stuff she'd brought with her on the side table. "You're my nephew, and family takes care of family around here. I'm also your new neighbor. Neighbors take care of each other, too. You're not going home with that injury. I'll be taking care of you until you're ready to travel."

Cole sent me an alarmed glance that made me grin back at him.

My mother might have some arthritis, but she was still spunky as hell.

He wasn't going to win this argument without having my mother bodily thrown out of the hospital.

"You're not going to win this one, so just give it up," I told my cousin.

"I brought you dinner," my mother fussed. "Hospital food isn't going to be enough for a man your size, Cole."

He hid it well, but I saw a spark of interest in his eyes for a brief second.

Hell, he was definitely a Remington male who loved food, whether he wanted to admit it or not.

"I'm going to heat up your food and feed you, and then your nurse is going to give you something for pain that will help you sleep.

"Millie," Cole said in a pained voice. "I'm fine. I'm not dying."

My mother ignored him as she took some containers from the bag and marched out of the room.

"Is she always like this?" he asked in a strained voice after my mother left the room.

"Always," I warned him. "She's going to get her way. Roll with it."

"I don't need her here," he said irritably.

I had to disagree.

My mother and the rest of his family was exactly what Cole needed.

He'd just been alone for so long that he didn't think he needed anyone, and I doubted that Asher was the only family he needed.

I did have to admit that the two of them had thrived though.

They'd had no family.

No support.

Yet the two of them had been as successful as the rest of the Remington men from our generation.

"She's not leaving unless you have her thrown out," I informed him. "She's stubborn as hell."

He looked annoyed as he answered, "I can't do that. Maybe we don't know each other well, but she is my aunt and she's trying to help."

Yep! There's definitely a decent guy beneath Cole's rough exterior.

"It's one night, and you'll sleep through it," I reminded him. "Let her fuss over you. She's an excellent cook. You'll like the food a lot better than what you'll get here."

It was almost amusing that Cole seemed to have no idea what to do with a motherly figure who wanted to fuss over his injury.

It was also kind of…sad.

Maybe I'd thought it was a pain in the ass at times because my parents had always worried about us with so much enthusiasm. But as an adult, I could appreciate the love and care we'd gotten as kids.

Cole and Asher had never had that.

Most likely, they'd always been in survival mode when they were younger.

"What do you think she made for dinner?" he asked grudgingly.

I already knew what she'd made.

I'd just never had a chance to eat it.

I was positive the rest of my family had already gotten fed when they arrived home from Billings.

"Chicken and dumplings with homemade biscuits," I informed him as I glanced into the bag she'd left behind. "And a large piece of huckleberry pie for dessert. She probably took the ice cream with her so she could put it in the freezer."

His face lit up a little. "It's been a long time since I've had huckleberry pie."

I clamped him lightly on the shoulder. "You're going to get something good out of letting her stay. She'll fuss over you, but you'll get used to it."

"I doubt that," Cole grumbled.

"Just let her do it," I requested. "She's been worried about you and Asher for years."

"Just this once," he relented reluctantly. "And I'm only doing it because I'm starving."

"You're a good man," I told him as my mother breezed back into the room.

"Most people think I'm a murderer," he said bitterly in a voice only loud enough for me to hear.

"We don't. We never did," I said, keeping my tone quiet, too."

"Go home, Devon," my mother insisted. "I left your food at your house, and Reese needs you."

The nurse came into the room to administer Cole's medication, and I heard Cole mutter softly, "You're going to owe me for this one, too."

I shot him a look that told him I had no problem with that.

I already owed my cousin everything for what he'd done for Reese.

"We'll pick you up tomorrow," I told him as I headed for the door. "We'll fly in the helicopter so it will be a smoother ride."

I ducked out of the room before Cole could argue, knowing my mother had the situation under control.

As soon as I left the hospital, every thought I had turned to Reese.

Even though she was surrounded by my family right now, I knew she needed me after what she'd been through.

I tried not to think about the fact that there would be a day sometime soon when she probably wouldn't need me anymore.

She'd be getting her old life back, and she'd finally be able to live without the fear of Kline trying to find her anymore.

I immediately shoved that thought out of my head.

She still needed me *right now,* and my gut wrenched at the thought of not being there for her.

She'd almost died today, and she'd had to face the man who had been wanting her dead for a long time.

I'd ridden with Reese and Cole to the hospital in my helicopter, but Kaleb had driven my truck here to Billings for me.

Kaleb and Anna had hitched a ride back to Crystal Fork with Lauren.

I'd sent my helicopter and my pilot back to the airstrip in Crystal Fork so the helipad would be clear for other emergencies.

As soon as I got outside I sprinted toward my truck.

Reese would hate it, but I knew I'd be driving like a bat out of hell to get home.

Chapter 26

Reese

"My jet is on the way to Spokane," Devon told me as we cuddled on the sofa later that evening after all of his family had departed. "He's bringing your parents here in the morning. They're pretty excited to see you."

I lifted my head from his shoulder, my face astonished as I stared at him. "I need to let them know."

One of the first things I'd done after we'd gotten Cole to the hospital was to call my mom and dad. I'd blubbered like a baby as I'd spoken to them.

It had felt like every emotion I'd try to shove deep inside me had come tumbling out all at the same time.

My mother had sobbed openly with joy as we spoke.

She'd sounded so relieved that I couldn't help but feel a large amount of guilt for putting my parents through this ordeal.

I'd rarely seen my father cry, but I could tell he was choking on tears as he'd assured me that they were both fine.

I'd been an emotional mess by the end of that phone call, but I'd told my parents I'd call them in the morning.

I'd expected to have to fly to Spokane as soon as possible. I desperately needed to hug my parents.

"No need," he explained. "I already talked to them while you were getting facial bone X-rays in the ER. They both wanted to get to you as soon as possible, and I knew you'd want the same. They actually liked the idea of coming here. Your dad said he'd always wanted to visit Montana, but he was a little baffled about the private jet."

Of course my parents had been surprised. They were wealthy, but not private jet wealthy.

"What did you tell him about who you were? I never had the chance to tell them about any of my life here. I was going to do that in person."

He shrugged. "I told him I was one of the many people who cared about you here in Crystal Fork. I figured you hadn't gotten around to telling him that I'm the guy you have wild sex with every chance we get."

I laughed and smacked him on the shoulder playfully. "I wouldn't tell my parents about *that* under any circumstances." I hesitated a second before I added, "Thank you. I really need to see them right now. I want to see for myself that they're doing okay. My dad mentioned that they'd both decided to retire a few months ago."

It probably wasn't unusual that Devon had anticipated my needs and taken care of everything. He was just that thoughtful of a guy, and he was used to taking charge of things."

"Marta and Kevin both sound like great people," Devon said.

"They are," I confirmed, surprised that he was on a first name basis with my parents. "Just how long of a conversation did you have with my parents?"

He grinned. "Long enough to find out that they both love to fish and to tell them that Kaleb has a river on his property full of fish to catch."

"They'd both love that," I said with a sigh. "Would you mind if they stayed here for a little while?"

I'd just given up my apartment recently and moved everything here to Devon's house because he'd informed me that I was never going back to staying by myself.

I hadn't argued with him about that because I really hadn't wanted to be alone in my apartment anymore.

Devon's home was the only place I had to offer my parents for accommodations.

"Did you really just ask me that question?" he asked with mock indignation. "This has been your home, too, Reese. Of course they can stay as long as they want. I'm looking forward to getting to know both of them. I want them to stay."

"Thank you," I said gratefully.

I could hardly believe that I'd finally be seeing my parents in a matter of hours. "I can't believe it's really over," I shared with him.

"It's over," he grumbled. "No more hiding. No more using an identity that isn't your own. No more fear of some asshole wanting to kill you."

All of that really hadn't sunk in yet for me.

"It's going to take me a while to get used to that," I admitted. "It feels like I've been in hiding forever."

"Do you think you'll be going home with your parents?" he asked in a cautious voice.

Devon and I had never talked about a future together.

We'd been living day by day for the most part.

I'd never been quite sure if our relationship was going to have an expiration date.

I had no doubt that I was head-over-heels in love with Devon, but I wasn't entirely sure that he felt the same way about me.

I shook my head. "I'd like to stay for a while. I'm not leaving Hannah when she's so close to her due date, and she doesn't have time to train and replace me at the moment. I'd like to handle that for her."

"I'm sure she'll appreciate that," he commented lightly.

Okay, he hadn't said anything about me staying permanently.

Did that mean he expected me to go back to Spokane?

I was mentally and physically wiped out, and I wasn't sure I could ask him that question right now.

I'd always known that this relationship might not be a forever thing, but I wasn't sure how I'd go through a life without Devon in it anymore.

Just the thought of that made my heart hurt.

We could probably do a long-distance thing, but that would be difficult for me.

Devon was anything but a casual boyfriend for me now.

He probably never had been.

I'd been crazy about him even when I'd offered him a friends with benefits relationship.

Now…he was my everything.

Relax, Reese. You don't know what's going to happen in the future yet.

"It's not like I have a job to go back to," I mumbled. "I'm going to have to find a new job."

Devon stroked a soothing hand over my back. 'One step at a time, sweetheart. It's going to take time to adjust back to your old life and identity."

I took a deep breath and let it out. I'd been living day to day for a while now. I could keep on doing it a little longer.

He was right. Everything felt off for me right now. I could go back to Spokane and pick up my old life with a new job change, but that just didn't appeal to me anymore.

Not only was I in love with a man who lived in Crystal Fork, but I'd become close to so many of the people who resided here.

I'd called two of my closest friends in Spokane.

They had been concerned about me, and we'd spoken like old friends, but they'd moved on with their lives.

It had been a year since the shooting, and I'd been gone for a long time.

One of them was engaged now, and the other had a new guy in her life.

While I'd always be close to them, I didn't feel the same bond that I did now with Hannah, Lauren, and Anna.

If I had to leave my life here in Montana, it was going to tear my heart out.

"You're thinking too much," Devon said as he dropped a kiss on top of my head. "Relax."

"I should be relaxed, right?" I questioned him. "It's over, and that's something I've desperately wanted for a long time."

"Today was traumatic," he argued. "Of course you're not relaxed. It's not like they apprehended the asshole, and you never had to see him again."

"I feel horrible about what happened to Cole," I said remorsefully.

"He'll live," Devon said drily. "Although he might be unhappy about having his doting aunt by his side all the time."

I smiled. He'd already told me about Millie's determination to nurse Cole back to health. "But he'll eat well, and he needs his family. Cole might have an abrasive personality, but he's a good man, Devon. I'll be his friend for life, whether he wants it or not. He saved my life."

"Which is exactly why I'll owe him for the rest of my life," Devon told me. "I should have been with you—"

"Don't start," I said as I put a finger on his lips. "I was on your mother's property. Nobody knew he was coming here. There's no way you could be with me every minute of every day, and I was in a safe place. It was a freak occurrence that he just happened to pull into town at the exact moment that I was close enough to be seen from the road. It's over, Devon, and Burke is the only one who died. Let it go."

"Not going to happen," he muttered. "Seeing that bastard with a gun pointed in your direction is going to haunt my nightmares for a long time."

"You protected me," I reminded him. "I don't think there's another person in the world that could have taken me down and covered my body as quickly as you did."

"Pure panic," he insisted. "Natural instinct."

"Everything you did saved my life, too. You came after me. Ralph was there at exactly the right moment to take Burke down."

"Kaleb said he was here to grill you about everything that happened," Devon said in an unhappy tone.

"I don't think he had a choice," I mused. "He needed to justify the fact that he killed the bad guy. He's going to be at the hospital bright and early to interview Cole, too. Maybe this is horrible, but

I'm glad he's dead. Kyle was completely innocent, and he had so much to offer patients who needed his help. He was also one of the most kindhearted friends I've ever had. Maybe some of it is selfish, too. The boogieman is gone and not just in a different location in prison."

"Hell, I'm glad he's dead, Reese. I wouldn't expect you to feel any other way."

God, that was one of the reasons I loved this man.

Even when I had feelings that were against my nature, Devon made me feel like they were completely normal.

He never judged anything I thought or did.

"Do you want another glass of wine?" he asked as he nodded his head at the empty glass on the coffee table.

I shook my head.

All I wanted to do was forget what had happened today.

"I think I'm ready for bed. I could use a good distraction," I murmured suggestively as I nuzzled his neck.

If tonight, tomorrow, or the next few weeks was all I'd ever have with Devon, I didn't want to waste a single moment of it.

I wanted to be skin-to-skin with this man and savor the way I always felt when I was with him.

"Reese, it was a long day for you…" his voice trailed off, and I knew he was trying to do what was best for me.

I kissed him, a long, slow, sensual kiss that told him exactly what I needed.

"I want to be with you, Devon," I said as I got on my knees and rested my forehead against his. "Do you really have a problem with that?"

"Fuck, no!" he said as he wrapped his arms tightly around me. "There's never going to be a time when I don't want exactly the same thing."

"Then take me to bed and make me forget everything that happened today. You're the only man who can. Make love to me."

I didn't have to ask twice.

Devon rose and swept me up into his arms, carried me upstairs, and gave me exactly what I wanted.

Chapter 27

Devon

I'd never been a guy who experienced things that were deeply emotional for me very often, but seeing Reese reunited with her parents had almost broken me.

All of the tears that had been shed by Reese and her parents had been happy tears of joy, but I could see the emotional toll Reese's nightmare experience had taken on all of them on their faces.

I knew Reese felt guilty for doing what she'd had to do, and the relief on her face when she'd seen her parents again and knew for sure that they were okay was almost my undoing.

It made my gut ache to think about the agony she'd endured day after day here in Crystal Fork knowing that her parents were probably frantic.

The three of them had chattered nonstop on the way home from the airstrip, and Reese hadn't hesitated to tell her parents that she was living with me and that I was an important man in her life.

I liked her parents tremendously.

They were kind.

They were intelligent.

And it was very apparent that they adored and loved their only child.

They'd spent the entire day catching up, and I'd tried not to intrude, but Reese had made sure that I was included in the conversation.

I'd driven them around the area, and they'd insisted on coming with me to pick up Cole and my mother at the hospital so they could thank both of them for helping to keep their daughter safe.

We'd finally gotten around to dinner, and I was about to put steaks on the grill while the women were inside preparing some side dishes.

Kevin strolled out of the sliding door with two bottles of beer in his hands and closed the door behind him. "Need some help?" he offered. "I'm pretty good at barbecuing a steak."

I grinned at the older man. "I think I can manage."

Reese looked a lot like her mother, but I'd been told that her auburn hair was definitely something she'd inherited from her father.

Kevin was gray now, but he was still extremely fit for a man his age.

He and Marta lived a very active life, even though they'd finally decided to retire.

He twisted the cap off my beer and handed it to me before he opened his own.

"I want to thank you for everything you and your family have done for Reese," he said in a genuine tone. "And maybe this is a little nosy or presumptuous, but I guess I want to know what your future intentions are toward my daughter. Lord knows she's been running her own life for a long time, but she's my only child. We've spent months worrying about her, and now I'd like to see her happy."

My grin got wider. I couldn't blame him for asking, and I was honest when I answered, "I don't know. That's up to Reese. I love her. I want to marry her and share a life with her, but I'm not sure that's what *she* wants. Her life has always been in Spokane, and you and Marta are there. My business is here, and so is my family, but I'd be willing to do whatever's necessary to be with your daughter."

I didn't see any reason to beat around the bush with him.

He'd almost lost Reese not once, but twice now.

He was protective of his only child, and he definitely wanted to know that I hadn't been taking advantage of her because she'd been in a vulnerable situation.

That *was* what I wanted, and he'd been a father half out of his mind with worry for the last year.

He had a right to be nosy and presumptuous at the moment because he wanted to protect Reese, and I respected that.

He smiled at me ruefully. "That's probably all I need to know. She's dated a few guys who didn't deserve her, but it's fairly obvious to me that you respect her. I just wanted a little reassurance after everything she's been through in the last year. I can't say that I planned on her getting serious with a billionaire someday, but I wanted something better for her than what she's dated previously."

"They were idiots," I grumbled. "They didn't appreciate the amazing woman they had. And she couldn't care less about my money. She's not impressed with my material success."

Kevin laughed. "I'm her dad, so I obviously agree with you. I know Reese. All she's ever wanted was a man who loved her."

"She's got that," I assured him.

"You make her happy, Devon," he observed before he took a long swig of his beer and swallowed. "You've gone through some tough times together already, so I don't think you're going to have any problems with future challenges."

I shrugged. "We started off as friends."

He nodded approvingly. "That makes the best kind of relationship. Marta and I were friends in medical school. I was a blockhead. It took me a year or so to realize that I was crazy about her. You two apparently caught on a lot faster than we did."

"Did you retire because you wanted to?" I asked Kevin curiously. "Or because you were so worried about Reese that you couldn't function?"

"A little of both," he said truthfully. "We've always planned to travel the world, and we aren't getting any younger. Neither one of us regrets our retirement. We both agreed that it was time. We've also thought about relocating to a place where we could slow down a little and enjoy a community. If Reese decides she wants to stay here, I don't think Marta and I would mind living in Crystal Fork when we aren't off exploring the world."

My heart started to beat a little faster as I searched his expression. "You'd be willing to move here?"

"There's nothing keeping us from moving," he informed me. "And I'd like to be close to my daughter and my grandchildren during my retirement years. I know Marta feels the same way."

Christ! He'd just given me one of the best gifts I could get.

I was certain they'd grow to love Crystal Fork and the people here, but...

I shook my head. "I'm not really sure that Reese wants to marry me and move to Crystal Fork. Her life is in Spokane."

He waved a hand in the air dismissively. "I think she belongs here now," he told me. "She talks about everyone here like they're family, and she's definitely in love with that horse you gave her. I don't see a single sign that she's missing Spokane. For what it's worth, she's crazy about you. I've never seen her this way with another man. I can tell by the way she looks at you. The only way you're going to know is to ask her yourself, Devon. I'm surprised you haven't gotten around to that yet."

"Maybe I was worried that I wouldn't get the answer I wanted," I joked.

"You have to ask the questions, son. You can't get any answers at all unless you do."

Kevin's answer was so much like something my father would have said that it surprised me.

"If I did decide to ask," I said hesitantly. "Do I have your blessing to marry your daughter?"

Hell, I knew it was more than a little old-fashioned to ask that question but considering all that he'd been through in the last year, it seemed like the right thing to do.

Kevin chuckled. "My daughter is a strongminded woman just like her mother. She's going to do what she wants to do. But if you plan to try to make her happy for the rest of your life, I'm all for it."

"That's the plan," I told him. "If she'll have me."

"Hey," Reese said as she opened the slider. "Where's the steaks. We're about done in here and we're hungry."

I turned and looked at the teasing smile on her face.

She was dressed in a pair of shorts that showed off her sexy legs and a sleeveless crop top because it was a warm summer day.

Reese looked different today, but it wasn't the clothes she was wearing.

It was the relaxed smile she wore on her face.

Gone was some of the stress that I'd seen for months, and she just looked...happy.

"You haven't even started?" she asked in a mock chastising voice.

"Just warming up the grill," I bullshitted.

"We were just discussing the best way to cook an exceptional steak," her dad said as he winked at me.

"Over a beer," she said with a laugh.

I had a feeling that Reese knew that her dad was grilling *me* and not the steaks, and she was trying to rescue me.

"We're good," I told her, sending her a glance that told her that I was fine chatting with her father. "It won't take long."

"What are you two cooking up in there?" her father asked.

Reese sent her father an adoring smile. "Potatoes, sweet corn, and salad. I made a hummingbird cake for Devon because it's his favorite."

I put a hand over my chest and rubbed it without consciously realizing what I was doing.

Hell, I'd never get used to the fact that Reese didn't think twice about doing something nice for me just because she wanted to do it.

I'd discovered that the cake wasn't exactly something she could whip up without going to a lot of trouble.

"One of my favorites, too," my father reminded Reese.

"Then I guess you two will have to fight over it," she said with a bright smile right before she closed the slider and went back to the kitchen.

Kevin nodded at my hand on my chest. "I guess you're not accustomed to having a woman do something for you just because she wants to make you happy."

I shook my head as I started to put the steaks on the grill. "Never had one who wanted to before," I admitted. "Maybe because I have enough money that I can order anything I want from anywhere in the world."

"It's not the same as something given to you from the heart," Kevin said as he reached for the steak spices to help me out.

"I discovered that the first time she made that cake," I answered. "You raised an amazing woman."

"That part was mostly her mom," Kevin said with a chuckle.

I doubted that.

I was fairly certain that Reese's strength and her character had been a combination of both of her parents.

Not that kids coming from a good family always turned out like Reese, but it certainly didn't hurt.

Kevin and I argued good-naturedly about exactly how a good grilled steak was achieved.

He gave in to my secret spices.

I gave in when he insisted on napping the steaks to make them juicier and more flavorful.

When we were finally ready to eat, the dinner turned out to be one of the most entertaining meals I'd ever experienced.

Reese, on the other hand, wasn't so thrilled when her mother started telling all of her embarrassing childhood stories.

But I enjoyed every moment of it since my mom had told more than enough of mine to Reese.

I was generous and shared the hummingbird cake.

I did, after all, plan to have the baker of that cake with me for a lifetime.

Reese Monroe *was* going to be mine.

All I had to do now was get her to agree to marry my sorry ass.

Chapter 28

Reese

"It feels really weird getting naked with a man when my parents are in the same house," I said with a giggle as I stripped off my bathing suit.

My parents had taken a swim with us and soaked in Devon's large-enough-to-have-a-party hot tub.

My mom and dad had gone off to their own suite of rooms Devon had put them in, and we'd headed to bed.

We always showered after being in the pool or hot tub to wash off the chlorine.

He sent me a shit-eating grin as he stripped off his swim trunks. "Why do you think I put them on the other side of the house? It's a big house with plenty of walls between us."

"It's a ridiculously large house," I said in a mock exasperated tone. "I'm not saying they can hear us, it just feels…weird. It's never happened before."

All in all, today had been one of the best days of my life.

My parents were here.

Devon was here.

And I was finally able to be Reese Monroe again.

My parents seemed to like Devon a lot, and vice versa.

But being with him like this with my family made the indecisiveness of our future even more difficult to bear.

What was I going to do if he decided he didn't want a future together?

Stop, Reese! None of that needs to be decided right now!

Except…it was getting hard to convince myself of that anymore.

I was cherishing every moment we had, but I couldn't help thinking about the fact that if he didn't want us forever, it was going to crush my soul.

I wrapped my arms around his neck when we were both naked and he turned on the shower. "Have I thanked you for everything you're doing for me and my parents?"

"Yes," he growled. "And if you thank me one more time for something that I want to do, I'm going to smack that beautiful ass of yours."

My brows rose and I shot him a sultry smile. "I think I might like that. So, thank you again."

He opened the door to the enormous shower. "Get in," he demanded.

I stepped into the elaborate shower.

The stall had multiple shower heads, bench seats, and enough room to fit an entire sports team.

It was obvious that Devon was in his bossy mood, and molten heat flooded between my thighs as he stepped into the shower.

There was an intense look in his dark eyes that was hard for me to read right now.

He wrapped his arms around my body and pulled our bodies as tightly together as they could get before he kissed me.

The embrace was rough, possessive, passionate, and demanding.

And my body responded with the same emotions.

It felt like Devon was trying to claim my mouth as well as the rest of my body.

It was a kiss like no other I'd ever shared with him before, but it felt almost…desperate, and his desperation called to my own.

B. A. Scott

Steam rose all around us, and I could almost imagine that it was the two of us that had created our environment, even though I knew it was coming from the moisture and heat of the water.

We weren't in one of the direct streams of water, but our bodies were slick with moisture as his hands roamed everywhere.

Again, I felt like he was trying to claim me, memorize every curve of my body, and I moaned against his mouth as I ran my hands over his slick skin in the same way.

I slid my hand down to grip his cock, but he grabbed my wrist and jerked our lips apart. "Don't," he insisted.

Our eyes met as he stroked his palm down my belly and did exactly what he didn't allow me to do.

The moment his fingers found and stroked my pussy; my legs almost gave way.

Devon knew how to pleasure a woman all too well, and he wasn't playing around today.

He stroked my clit until my body was ready to implode, but he suddenly stopped, turned my body around, and placed my hands on one of the bench seats.

He leaned over me until his mouth was near my earlobe.

He nipped it and then said in a wicked voice. "Tell me you want my cock, Reese. Tell me exactly what you need."

I was so aroused, and I wanted him so much that I blurted out, "I want your cock inside me so badly, Devon. Fuck me."

"I think I promised you this," he said hoarsely as he smacked my ass.

I was so startled that my body jerked.

He hadn't hurt me.

In fact, that brief sting made my core clench hard with need.

"Are you going to tell me you're sorry again?"

"I'm sorry," I said immediately.

He put his hand between my thighs and stroked my clit like a man on a mission.

It was like he wanted to make sure that I still…needed him.

That I still wanted him.

God, he should know the answers to those questions by now, but there was definitely an intensity to Devon that I'd never experienced before.

Because I didn't know what our future was going to be together, things between the two of us felt just as intense for me.

I threw my head back and moaned his name.

He slapped my ass again, and the pleasure was so extreme that I nearly lost my mind.

An instant later, he buried himself to his balls inside me, and I let out a choked sob of relief.

I needed this.

I needed *him*.

I needed the satisfying pleasure of our bodies fused together this way.

He grasped my hips and started to fuck me hard, and I pushed my hips back meeting every stroke.

He fucked me like a man who had completely lost control, and I savored every commanding thrust.

"Oh, God! Devon!" I cried out, my body craving release, yet wanting to stretch the pleasure out for a little longer.

Suddenly, he pulled me up, turned me around, and grabbed my ass to lift me up.

I wrapped my legs around him automatically.

"Not like that. Not this time," he said huskily as he pushed my back against the wall.

I wrapped my arms around his neck, sighing at the feel of our naked bodies sliding together.

He was inside me in an instant, and his lips claimed mine.

My legs tightened around his waist, wanting to get as close as possible to this man that I loved so damn fiercely.

He pummeled into me as he gripped my ass tightly, holding me in place.

I panted as he released my lips.

"You're mine, Reese. Fucking say it before I lose my mind," he said gruffly beside my ear.

"I'll always be yours, Devon," I said mindlessly.

"Fuck knows I'm already yours," he said, his chest heaving.

He reached his hand between our bodies and expertly stimulated my clit.

That sent me over the edge almost immediately.

"Yes, yes, yes," I chanted as my climax tore through my body with so much power that it was almost terrifying.

My core spasmed violently while Devon kept fucking me like a madman.

He let out a tormented groan as he came deep inside me.

"I love you," I whimpered before I could stop the words from leaving my lips. "I love you so much that it hurts."

Already spent, Devon's body suddenly froze.

He gripped me tighter, but he didn't move for a moment.

Tear sprang to my eyes because he hadn't said it back to me.

Dammit! I shouldn't have let those words leave my mouth, but it was something I just couldn't hold back anymore.

I did love him and not telling him how I felt had been pure agony for me.

Obviously, he hadn't been ready to go there.

I couldn't regret blurting out how I felt, but the pain in my chest because he obviously couldn't say those words to me was excruciating.

Once I'd caught my breath, he slowly lowered my feet to the ground, grabbed the body wash and quickly washed our bodies and rinsed us off before he turned off the shower.

Embarrassed, I jumped out of the shower before he did and grabbed a towel.

He took the towel from me and thoroughly dried me off before he swiped the same towel over his body.

I ran a brush through my hair as he was drying himself.

"Did you mean that?" he asked hesitantly. "Or was that just a heat of the moment thing?"

I could easily tell him that the words had slipped during an orgasmic moment, but I wasn't about to lie to him now.

"I've been wanting to tell you that for a long time," I confessed.

He wrapped his arms around my nude body. "Tell me again now that I'm over the shock and I know that you mean it."

Okay, so maybe his sudden freeze hadn't been exactly as I'd interpreted it.

"I love you," I said simply. "I have for a long time, but it just seemed too soon to say those words, and I wasn't in a position to have anything more until my situation was resolved. Maybe I was also a little afraid that you really didn't want to hear those words."

He picked me up, carried me to the bed, and sat me down on the sheets gently.

"You're definitely stuck with me now," he said as he got into bed and pulled me close to him.

"Why?" I asked, confused.

"Because I love you, too, Reese Monroe, and now that I know that you love me, I'm never planning on ever letting you go."

Chapter 29

Reese

My eyes filled with tears.
Had he really just said those words to me?
I'd hoped…

I'd wanted…

I'd dreamed…

But now that Devon had actually said that he loved me, I felt like my heart was going to explode.

"Hey," he said softly. "Being stuck with me isn't going to be *that* bad."

I knew that he hated to see me cry, but I felt so emotional that I couldn't stop the tears from falling no matter how hard I tried.

"When you didn't say the words back to me right away, I was afraid that you didn't feel the same way," I told him. "I was afraid."

He pulled me into his lap and started to rock my body. "I'm so sorry, sweetheart. I was shocked. I had the same fears. I knew what I wanted and how I felt. I was afraid that you didn't feel the same way about me, too. I'm an idiot. I should have said those words back to you right away."

God, we were both idiots.

My heart had always told me that he had to be feeling the same way I was, but my insecurities had kept me from blurting out those words before today.

"Marry me, Reese," he said gruffly. "Be my wife and put me out of my misery."

"Is that an order or are you asking?" I teased; my heart so full of joy that I wasn't sure it could take this much happiness. Especially after the pain and fear of the last year.

Of course I wanted to marry him.

"I'm asking," he admitted. "I don't have a ring, but I'm definitely asking. We'll pick out the ring together. I'll do everything in my power to make you happy."

I leaned my head back so I could look at him.

Everything I'd ever hoped for was there in those gorgeous dark eyes.

"Yes," I said simply as another tear dropped onto my cheek. "I'll pick out my own ring. You'd pick something outrageous. I want something small."

"Big," he argued. "I want every man out there to know that I was already smart enough to snap up the best woman on the planet."

"Medium," I compromised. "It would be hard for me to wear a thousand-pound rock at work all the time, and it's not my style."

"Deal," he said with a grin.

"I'm going to have to sell my place in Spokane, but you have a private jet that can get me to my parents often."

"You want to stay here?" Devon asked hopefully.

I nodded. "I do. I hate leaving my parents in Spokane without me, but everything and everyone else I love is here. I'll still be able to see them. It's a short flight."

"Can you get your license to practice here?"

"It will take a while, but that's okay. I'd like to help Hannah through the first months of her pregnancy," I told him. "She's not going to want to be at the office, and I need to hire a replacement for myself."

"You might not have to be without your parents," he said with humor in his voice. "Your dad already mentioned that he might be interested in moving to Montana. He said he and Marta want to travel a lot, but he wants to be here in his retirement to be close to you and the grandbabies we're apparently going to give him."

I really wanted to have a child or two, but I wasn't sure how Devon felt about kids.

"I want to have your child," I shared with him. "But I'm not sure what you want."

"After watching what Tanner is going through right now, I'm sure I'm going to be losing my shit, but I'd like the same thing," he said as he swiped the teardrop from my face. "But I'd really prefer that you were never uncomfortable or in pain again. That's my only real hesitation."

"It would be worth it to bring our child into the world," I assured him. "I've assisted in tons of deliveries over the years. It's not like I don't know what's going to happen."

"Are you going to be happy here?" he asked pensively. "I could relocate to Spokane. It wouldn't be the easiest transition, but I'd figure it out."

There was a stunned moment of silence.

All of Devon's business interests were here, and so was all of his family.

He'd have to give up this beautiful, custom-built home and the people he cared about in Crystal Fork.

The fact that he'd offered to leave all of that just to be with me was almost unbelievable.

Or…maybe it wasn't.

He wanted to make sure I was happy, just like I wanted him to be happy.

I wasn't sure when I was ever going to get used to a guy who put me first in his life.

"You'd do that for me?" I said with astonishment in my voice. "Everything you love is here in Montana."

He shrugged. "If you wanted or needed to be somewhere else, I'd be there with you. I could work remote."

"I want to be here," I reassured him. "It feels like home to me now, and I couldn't imagine living anywhere else. If my parents end up moving here, that would be the icing on the cake."

"When are you going to marry me?" Devon asked as he rear-ranged our bodies until we were lying next to each other on the bed with his arms tightly around my waist.

I snuggled close to him and buried my face in his neck. "I guess that depends on how large of a wedding you want."

"I couldn't care less about the size of the wedding. I'm just hoping it can happen soon."

"How soon?" I asked curiously.

"A few weeks?" he asked hopefully.

I snorted. "We'd have to run off to Vegas, but I'm not opposed to that. I've never really liked being the center of attention."

"Not good enough for you," he said huskily. "And you need to be the center of attention for once. Destination wedding in Hawaii or Bali with a honeymoon in Galapagos?"

I shook my head. "That's not going to happen quickly. Hannah can't travel with the baby until she's old enough to build up some immunities. Let's get married here. I could plan a nice wedding and reception right here on your property."

"It's going to be elaborate," he warned. "Everything you've always wanted for your wedding."

"I already have the thing I wanted the most," I told him.

"What?"

"The right guy who loves me," I teased.

When he lifted my chin and kissed me, I felt like everything was suddenly right in my life.

Everything had shifted into place after a year of chaos.

He finally released my lips and ended the tender embrace. "I have a private jet, Reese. If you want to go someplace more romantic for our honeymoon, I can take you anywhere in the world that you want to go."

My heart tripped as I saw the sincerity in his gaze.

"Galapagos is perfect. I want to share it with you," I said softly. "But there's no feasible way this wedding will happen in two weeks. I need time to plan and get things together."

"You'll have an army of help," he promised. "Both family and professionals."

"Let me do some checking and see what date we can set. It would be nice if we could do it before the snow flies."

It was already summer, so that didn't leave me much time.

"I don't want you to feel like I'm rushing you," Devon said solemnly. "I just want you to be mine as soon as possible. I know exactly what I want, but I don't want to push you into this before you're ready."

I felt like I'd been waiting for Devon for a very long time.

I really didn't want to wait, either.

I'd learned the hard way that life was short. I didn't want to waste the opportunity to start my future with Devon.

"I don't have any doubts," I said. "I feel like I've always been waiting for you. I love you, Devon. I'm all for getting married sooner rather than later. I just need to see how soon we can pull this off."

"My first priority is to get my ring on your finger," he said hoarsely as he rolled me onto my back and pressed his upper body into mine.

I savored the moment as our gazes locked and held.

I could see the raw love and devotion in his gorgeous dark eyes.

Nothing was hidden anymore.

I was simply looking back at the man who I knew was going to love me for the rest of my life.

"For a man who's always avoided commitment, I'm surprised that you have no doubts," I told him breathlessly.

He grinned. "Maybe I didn't want to commit because I hadn't met you yet. You were the only woman who could make me change my mind."

I knew exactly why Devon had never wanted to commit, and I felt lucky that I was the one he'd trusted enough to break all of his rules.

"Should we take your parents to Billings tomorrow?" he asked. "Your dad seems to enjoy a beer or two. He might like the breweries."

"You're not going into work at all?" I asked.

Hannah had already insisted I take some time off to be with my mom and dad, but I hadn't expected Devon to take the entire day off.

"Nope," he informed me. "I probably won't go in most of the week, either. I'd like to spend some time getting to know your mom and dad. I covered for my brothers plenty when they were getting their romantic lives together. They can return the favor. Now that you're able to go anywhere you want, I'd like to show all of you some of my home state."

"I'd love that," I said with a sigh as I stroked the nape of his neck. "It still seems hard to believe that I can go anywhere I want and do anything I want. I can actually be *me* again, Devon. That's going to take some getting used to after the last year."

I let the fact that I was finally free seep into my soul.

Free to go roam to places I'd never been before.

Free to go back to my chosen career.

And free to love Devon without reservations because we could actually plan our future together now.

Our relationship wasn't in limbo anymore, and I couldn't wait to get on with our lives.

"I have a feeling you'll get used to it pretty quickly," he said, amused. "I'm going to take you to see anything you want to see this week. I'm just hoping you're not planning to go anywhere right now."

He kissed his way slowly along my jawline and down my neck.

My body responded instantly. "No plans for the next few hours," I said in a teasing voice.

"Good," he responded in a satisfied tone. "Because I have plans to occupy your time."

That was *exactly* what he did, and I didn't utter a single complaint.

Chapter 30

Devon

"How much longer is this going to take?" I said grumpily as we sat in a waiting room of a Billings hospital exactly one week later. "Do you think something is wrong?"

"No," Reese said in a calm voice. "I told you that it was probably going to take a while for Hannah to deliver. It's her first baby. Be patient. I don't think it will be much longer."

Hannah had gone into labor at four am this morning.

It was now after nine pm.

In my mind, that was *way* too long for any woman to suffer through labor.

We'd left a note for Reese's parents, grabbed a coffee, and headed to the hospital early this morning.

We'd already ordered takeout for breakfast, lunch, and dinner, and still no baby.

I looked around the waiting room, grateful that there didn't appear to be any other women in active labor because we were taking up most of the small waiting room.

Lauren was sitting with my mother and Hannah's mother, Joy, across from us.

Kaleb was sitting next to me with Anna on his other side.

The Remington clan was all here and ready for this baby to be born.

Tanner had been out to the waiting room a few times in Hannah's earlier stages of labor, and my brother looked like he'd aged ten years in a matter of hours.

He was frazzled, and I could tell that this entire childbirth thing was killing him.

"Tanner looks like hell," I said to Reese in a low voice.

She squeezed my hand. "No, he doesn't. He looks like any other expectant father waiting for his child to be born. Some guys manage it better than others, but it's not unusual for any of them to be a little anxious. This is a new experience for Tanner."

Anxious?

Tanner looked like he'd been dragged through hell and back.

"Hannah is extremely calm," Reese added. "She just wants this pregnancy to be over and to hold her little girl."

The women had been with Hannah for a while before she'd entered her final stages of labor.

Reese had been serene about this process all day and evening, so she obviously didn't think anything was wrong.

"Hannah feels like she's prepared," Joy said. "You helped her a lot with that, Reese. She doesn't seem anxious at all about the actual delivery. "

Reese smiled at the older woman. "You and Millie helped her more than I did. You've been through it. I've just helped deliver babies in the delivery room."

"I can't wait to see my first grandchild," Millie said excitedly. "My boys have made me wait forever for this day."

"Me, too," Joy said with a sigh. "How are the wedding preparations going, Reese?"

Okay, that topic distracted me a little.

We'd set the date for the first Saturday in October.

It wasn't that far away, but it still seemed too long to me.

"Good," Reese answered in an upbeat tone. "I thought it was going to be difficult, but Devon sent me so many specialists that I don't really have to do much but make the final decisions.

"I'm so excited that I'm going to be a bridesmaid," Lauren said enthusiastically.

"Me, too," Anna seconded. "The dresses we're looking at are pretty stunning."

Reese had asked Hannah to be her maid of honor.

I'd hired a dress designer for all the women's dresses so they could get whatever they wanted.

Before Cole had left to return to Austin yesterday, I'd asked him to stand up for me to make the numbers even.

Surprisingly, he'd agreed without much hesitation.

I had to wonder if my mother had softened him up on the idea of family. She'd been at his place most of the time that he'd been recovering, and she'd fed him so well that he'd complained about gaining some weight.

Reese had checked on Cole every single day, and she'd just ignored his complaints about her worrying too much about a minor injury.

She was slowly getting used to living her old life again. A life that was free of fear and hiding.

Most of the people in town knew about what had happened to her now and her real identity. The people who knew her and cared about her had been incredibly supportive and had offered to help her with the wedding.

Honestly, Reese hadn't needed my help all that much to get things started for the wedding. She had so many family members and friends to help her that it was probably overwhelming.

She asked my opinion on most things, but I agreed with whatever she seemed to want the most.

I didn't care how we ended up married, I just wanted it to happen.

I was glad now that I hadn't hauled her off to Vegas like I'd been tempted to do before I decided that she deserved better.

It would have been faster, but she would have missed all the normal bridal stuff and traditions that seemed important to her now that she was wedding planning.

When she was huddled with Hannah, Lauren, and Anna chattering about the wedding plans and the dresses, she just looked excited and…happy.

Just watching her during those moments made it worth the wait.

I glanced down at the ring I'd just put on her finger the night before.

I hadn't screwed around when it came to her ring. I'd wished that I'd had that ring to put on her finger the moment I asked her to marry me. I'd had a jeweler at the house on Monday, and I'd gotten the custom ring back yesterday afternoon.

I would have preferred something a little flashier, but Reese loved her engagement ring, so I'd learn to live with a smaller carat value than I would have liked.

"I haven't decided on a dress design yet," Reese told the women. "There's just so many options, and they're all beautiful."

"You'll know when you see that right design," Anna told her. "It will just feel like…you."

"I hope so," Reese answered. "It has to be made in a pretty short period of time."

My mother looked at me as she said, "When my sons find the right woman, they're impatient for that wedding. I never thought I'd see Devon this eager to get married. He could have given you a little more time."

Reese shook her head. "I'm good with it. I really don't want to get married in the middle of a Montana winter. We're already going to need outdoor heaters for every area we're using."

"It's going to be a lovely wedding," Mom said enthusiastically. "Although that will mean I won't have any more kids to nag about getting married."

"Thank God," Kaleb said in a relieved voice. "But I doubt that will stop you from nagging us about producing more grandchildren."

My mother smiled at him sweetly. "Not a chance. I'll be content for a little while with my new granddaughter, but I'm going to keep hoping for more. Especially from my oldest son. You're not getting any younger Kaleb, and neither am I."

Anna snickered from her place beside Kaleb, and her husband shot my mother an exasperated look.

"Anna and I haven't been married that long," Kaleb grumbled.

"You were married before Tanner," she reminded her eldest son. Kaleb folded his arms across his chest and stubbornly stayed silent. He already knew better than to try to argue with our mother.

I already knew his situation because we'd talked about it more than once lately.

I knew that Kaleb wanted to have a child and so did Anna, but he wasn't going to crush under our mother's pressure to make it happen any faster.

Anna still traveled a lot because she was an international pop star, and they were waiting until Anna could scale the travel and appearances back a little at a time.

They'd decide when it was the right time, and it wasn't going to happen any sooner because my mother thought it should.

The room got eerily quiet for an instant as everyone spotted Tanner coming toward the waiting room.

I grinned when I noticed that he was carrying his child in his arms. It was over.

"She's here," Joy and my mother squealed simultaneously.

Everyone was on their feet by the time Tanner carried his daughter into the waiting room.

"Hannah's fine," he announced. "Everyone, meet Winter Elizabeth Remington, my new daughter."

The extra ten years I'd seen on Tanner's face earlier had entirely vanished.

Now, he was grinning like a man who had never gone through an exhausting twenty-hour delivery.

It wasn't difficult to see that he was already completely in love with his new daughter.

Tanner was looking at Winter with complete and utter adoration.

I stood back a little and let my mother and Joy get their first glimpse of their new grandchild.

"She's beautiful," Reese said as she held my hand tightly.

I took a closer look. "She's wrinkled and red," I observed.

"Perfectly normal and healthy," Reese informed me. "I'm sure Hannah is elated."

Elated? Hell, I was certain she was exhausted and glad all the pain was over, too.

Honestly, Tanner looked ecstatic himself and so incredibly proud of the little girl he and Hannah had created.

As I looked at the joy on my brother's face, it suddenly hit me that I really did want this for myself someday.

I just didn't want the whole delivery part of the occasion.

That had looked brutal.

Kaleb and I both got our chance to slap Tanner on the back and congratulate him on his firstborn child.

My mother and Joy got a very brief opportunity to hold Winter.

"I have to get her back to Hannah," Tanner said as he lovingly took his daughter back from his mother.

We all hugged each other before we started to exit the hospital.

"Relieved?" Reese asked as we wandered toward my truck in the parking lot.

"Yeah," I admitted. "I was afraid Tanner was going to have a heart attack before all of this was over."

Reese chuckled. "They usually forget all about the anxiety once the baby is born. Tanner will be fine. He has Winter and Hannah to fuss over now that the delivery is over."

"Do you really want to go through all that?" I asked her seriously.

She leaned against the truck for a moment as she said, "I thought you wanted to have a child."

"I did," I blurted out. "I do. I just hate the thought of you going through all that pain and misery."

She laughed. "It's really not that bad, Devon. There are pain relief options, and most women feel fine during their pregnancy if there are no complications."

"Morning sickness?"

She wrapped her arms around my neck. "There are vitamins and medications for that if it's severe. I'm starting to think me being pregnant would be harder for you than it is for me. I know that Tanner was a lot more worried about this delivery than Hannah."

I put a hand on her flat abdomen. "I really want that for us someday, but it looks scary as fuck. You're my whole damn life now, Reese."

She reached out a hand and ran it lovingly over my jaw. "Nothing bad is going to happen to me if we have a child, Devon. All the pregnancy stuff we'll get through together. We're partners now, right? And by that time, I'll be your wife. You're just a little wary because you just watched your brother go through the whole experience. We aren't looking at a baby right away. Relax."

I calmed down a little.

She was right.

If we wanted a child someday, I was going to have to be there for her and not get caught up with every bad thing that could happen.

"I'm always going to worry about you," I warned her. "And I'll be a majorly possessive, obsessive pain in your ass as a husband."

She smiled. "Expected. You're already that way as a fiancé. I know who you are, Devon, and I'm still madly in love with you. Feeling better?"

I wrapped my arms tightly around her waist. "Yeah. I guess this entire day has been a little unnerving."

"But it had a very happy ending," she said with a sigh. "You have a beautiful new niece."

"She's your niece, too," I reminded her.

Maybe she wasn't *officially* an aunt, but she would be soon.

Her smile was suddenly radiant. "I know. I can't wait to hold her. We better get home so I can finish Winter's baby blanket that I'm crocheting tonight. I want to bring it in the morning so Hannah can use it to take her home."

"Hey," I said gruffly as she started to remove her arms from around my neck. "Aren't you forgetting something? Kiss me first."

Christ! I adored this woman and her desire to do things for other people, but there were going to be times when I had to remind her to be selfish occasionally.

Billionaire Undeceived

"I wasn't sure that you'd want me to do that in the middle of this parking lot," she said remorsefully.

Yeah, there were a few people coming and going, but I didn't give a shit.

"I do," I confirmed. "Right here. Right now. I'm always going to want you to kiss me, Reese, no matter who's watching."

Without a moment's hesitation, she pulled my head down until our lips met and laid a loving, passionate kiss on me that almost blew my mind.

"You're going to be in trouble for that when we get home," I growled after we'd surfaced for air.

"Counting on it," she said as she winked at me and removed herself from my tight grip on her waist.

As I opened the passenger door for Reese, I knew my life was never going to be boring with her as my wife.

She was always going to challenge me and drive me crazy.

I was grinning as I jogged to the driver's side of my truck, deciding that harmony and peace were highly overrated.

Epilogue

Reese

The weeks that led up to my wedding with Devon flew by so fast that they were almost a blur.

In addition to all of the wedding plans, I'd had to make a trip to Spokane to clean out my home and put it up for sale.

Most of the hard work was done by movers at Devon's insistence, but I'd needed to decide what I was going to have sent to Crystal Fork and what I was going to donate.

Devon had come with me to Spokane, and I'd finally gotten a chance to fly in his very posh private jet for the first time.

Although his money had never mattered to me, I had to admit that there were certain perks to marrying a billionaire.

Our honeymoon and any future travel Devon and I did was going to be incredible.

His contacts and endless supply of professionals had helped me plan my wedding without a ton of stress.

I'd needed to get Montana licenses, both a driver's license and a license to practice as a nurse practitioner in the state of Montana. I hadn't received my license yet to practice as a medical professional here, but it should be arriving soon.

I wanted to open my own practice in Billings. I was also hoping that I could someday open a clinic for routine medical care for the residents in Crystal Fork. I'd probably need help from a physician to deal with the things I wasn't trained to handle, but I'd figure that out after I started my practice in Billings. Crystal Fork was a small town, but it would be nice if I could get the residents some kind of medical care, so they didn't have to travel to Billings for every minor issue. Not everyone here had easy access to Billings. Especially some of the senior residents in town.

Hannah had taken some much-needed time off to spend with Winter, and I'd hired and trained a very competent replacement for my management position at Glam Anywhere.

All of these things had been accomplished in such an abbreviated period of time that it made me a little dizzy just thinking about it.

Devon had been an enormous help, but he also reminded me when I needed to stop and take care of myself.

I'd continued on with my video counselor that Wyatt had mysteriously found for me.

I was able to tell her everything, and working through my previous trauma was helping me enormously.

I wasn't freezing up or cowering from things that used to be triggers for me.

I could watch a thunderstorm roll in and be amazed at the power of nature instead of seeing it as a threat of some kind.

I was becoming myself again, and there was no better feeling in the world for me.

My parents would be relocating to Crystal Fork permanently in about a month. They'd purchased a small hobby ranch with some property where my dad could have chickens, goats, and a dog or two.

My mom was thrilled that she'd finally have all the space she wanted for a greenhouse and a garden.

My parents had fallen in love with Crystal Fork just like I had, and they'd become fast friends with some of the residents already, especially Millie, Joy, Silas, and Charlie.

I let out a long, happy sigh.

My life felt so perfect that it was almost scary.

"That was a pretty big sigh for a woman who just got married," Devon said in a teasing voice as the two of us danced at our reception.

I'd had a fairytale wedding.

Devon had made sure that absolutely nothing was left out of our wedding.

He'd even had Kaleb bring Luna to me at the house so I could ride into the venue on horseback.

Luna had been decked out in fancy tack and flowers.

Maybe I was biased, but I thought she was the most beautiful horse I'd ever seen.

It had been a short ride to the area where our wedding ceremony had taken place and where my dad had been waiting for me to walk me down the aisle, but I thought the gesture was incredibly romantic.

Devon could claim that he wasn't a romantic all he wanted, but his actions always told me how much he loved me and wanted to please me.

It had been an unseasonably nice day, but all of the wedding and reception areas had still been heated to a comfortable temperature.

Anna had been right about my dress. Once I saw the dress I really wanted, I knew it was the one. It was a little simpler than some of the ones I'd looked at, but everything about the delicately embroidered lace dress had appealed to me.

I hadn't worn a huge veil. Just some simple lace that trailed down the back of my auburn hair.

"I was just thinking about how perfect my life feels right now. I just married the man of my dreams, and everyone I love is right here to help us celebrate."

I was also leaving on my dream honeymoon tomorrow to the Galapagos Islands.

I wanted to relish this perfect time in my life as long as possible.

Life was full of ups and down, and I knew there would be a lot of times in the future when life wouldn't be perfect.

Maybe I appreciated this day so much because I'd had a lot of those imperfect times in my life, especially during the last year.

Just months ago, I hadn't been able to envision meeting the perfect guy, getting married, and possibly having a child someday.

"That's kind of a low bar for perfection," Devon said jokingly. "Especially since you just married me. I'm definitely *not* perfect. Never will be."

I looked up at him as Devon led me around the dance floor.

God, the man looked amazing in a tuxedo.

"You're perfect for me," I told him softly.

He lowered his head and kissed me, and I let out another sigh when that tender embrace was over.

He'd probably always be self-mocking about his value as a husband, but I knew how lucky I was to have married a man like him.

As Devon turned me on the dance floor, I caught a glimpse of Lauren talking with Cole.

"Lauren looks uncomfortable whenever she's around Cole," I observed aloud.

Cole had just made his permanent move to Montana.

I still hadn't met Asher. He was following in another few weeks. He'd gotten a wedding invitation from us, but we'd never gotten a response.

While Cole might be warming up to family a little, Asher obviously wasn't going to be present at family gatherings anytime soon.

"Cole isn't exactly a warm and fuzzy guy," Devon reminded me. "He's basically an asshole. We know there's a decent human buried inside his body somewhere, but he's pretty rough around the edges."

I shook my head slowly. "I don't think that's the problem. Lauren can usually get along with anyone, even if they aren't exactly friendly. She's insightful and she connects with people wherever they are. She seems uneasy whenever he's around. I can sense it, and that's weird for her."

"It's not like they have some kind of bad history," Devon mused. "Lauren was still a child when Cole and Asher left Montana, and they haven't been back since then. Maybe she just doesn't like him."

Honestly, Cole wasn't the easiest guy to like, but I sensed it was more wariness than dislike coming from Lauren.

It was almost like she was fearful for some reason.

Lauren tried to hide it, and when she saw me looking her way, she smiled like she was having the time of her life.

I wasn't buying it though.

There was something about Cole that made her nervous.

But maybe Devon was right.

Maybe Cole was so intimidating because of his gruff demeanor that it made her uncomfortable, although I found that hard to believe because she'd put up with the Remington brothers most of her life.

In fact, she had no problem giving their bullshit right back to them.

I smiled back at Lauren and filed my thoughts away for a later time.

Eventually, I'd ask her why Cole made her nervous.

Lauren and I had gotten extremely close, but I knew she wasn't going to be honest with me right now because it was my wedding day. She'd blow off the question because she wouldn't want to talk about anything unpleasant today.

She'd actually fretted about being the only plain, chubby woman in my wedding party, which had made me crazy. She'd dieted and exercised like a madwoman over the last several weeks.

In reality, Lauren wasn't chubby, nor was she plain. She was naturally curvy. It was just the way her body was built. She lamented over the dimples in her cheeks, never realizing that when she smiled, her face was radiantly gorgeous.

I reminded myself that we were going to work on her self-esteem when I got back from my honeymoon.

She saw herself as an unattractive nerd, but I suspected she'd always felt that way because men were intimidated by her genius IQ and her intelligence.

She didn't need to diet like crazy or exercise like she was training for a marathon.

Lauren needed to accept herself as beautiful exactly the way she was, and I was going to help her do exactly that.

She didn't need to change a damn thing about her appearance, and she was one of the kindest women I knew.

I filed that thought away in my brain, too.

Lauren and I would talk when all of the craziness of my wedding and honeymoon was over.

"Are you excited about our honeymoon?" I asked Devon. "I can't wait to get to South America."

He tightened his arm around my waist. "I'll just be happy when we're alone and I can get you naked for the first time as my wife."

I swatted his shoulder playfully. "How can you be thinking about that when we're in the middle of our wedding reception?"

"Sweetheart, I've got news for you," he said in a husky voice. "I'm *always* thinking about that."

I laughed because I actually spent a significant amount of time thinking about getting him naked, too.

Probably way too much time.

"I guess it's about time for us to cut that beautiful cake," I said to Devon as the song ended.

We'd already eaten an incredible dinner, but Devon had insisted on getting a few dances in with his new bride before we cut the cake.

I reluctantly started to let him go, but he pulled me back against him.

"You're forgetting something, beautiful," he said as he caught my gaze. "Kiss me."

My heart tripped as I saw all of the emotions in his beautiful dark eyes.

Love.

Tenderness.

Commitment.

But one of the most obvious right now was his happiness.

Happiness looked so good on this man that I wanted to keep those gorgeous eyes filled with that emotion for the rest of my life.

Devon Remington had given me a huge gift when he'd given me his heart.

There would never be a day in our future that I wouldn't be grateful and try to be gentle with it.

I knew to the depths of my soul that he'd always do the same with mine.

My heart would always be safe with this man that I loved so utterly and completely.

I wrapped my arms tightly around his neck again and gave him exactly what we *both* wanted.

~The End~

Cole Remington's story, *Billionaire Unforgiven*,
will be released on February 26th, 2026.

Cole's book is now available for preorder!

Please visit me at:
http://www.authorjsscott.com
http://www.facebook.com/authorjsscott

You can write to me at
jsscott_author@hotmail.com

You can also tweet
@AuthorJSScott

Please sign up for my Newsletter for updates,
new releases and exclusive excerpts.

Books by J. S. Scott:

Billionaire Obsession Series

The Billionaire's Obsession~Simon
Heart of the Billionaire
The Billionaire's Salvation
The Billionaire's Game
Billionaire Undone~Travis
Billionaire Unmasked~Jason
Billionaire Untamed~Tate
Billionaire Unbound~Chloe
Billionaire Undaunted~Zane
Billionaire Unknown~Blake
Billionaire Unveiled~Marcus

Billionaire Unloved~Jett
Billionaire Unwed~Zeke
Billionaire Unchallenged~Carter
Billionaire Unattainable~Mason
Billionaire Undercover~Hudson
Billionaire Unexpected~Jax
Billionaire Unnoticed~Cooper
Billionaire Unclaimed~Chase
Billionaire Unreachable~Wyatt
Billionaire Unexplained~Kaleb
Billionaire Unforgettable~Tanner
Billionaire Undeceived~Devon

British Billionaires Series

Tell Me You're Mine
Tell Me I'm Yours
Tell Me This Is Forever

Sinclair Series

The Billionaire's Christmas
No Ordinary Billionaire
The Forbidden Billionaire
The Billionaire's Touch
The Billionaire's Voice
The Billionaire Takes All
The Billionaire's Secret
Only A Millionaire

Accidental Billionaires

Ensnared
Entangled
Enamored
Enchanted
Endeared

Walker Brothers Series

Release
Player
Damaged

The Sentinel Demons

The Sentinel Demons: The Complete Collection
A Dangerous Bargain
A Dangerous Hunger
A Dangerous Fury
A Dangerous Demon King

The Vampire Coalition Series

The Vampire Coalition: The Complete Collection
The Rough Mating of a Vampire (Prelude)
Ethan's Mate
Rory's Mate
Nathan's Mate
Liam's Mate
Daric's Mate

Changeling Encounters Series

Changeling Encounters: The Complete Collection
Mate Of The Werewolf
The Dangers Of Adopting A Werewolf
All I Want For Christmas Is A Werewolf

The Pleasures of His Punishment

The Pleasures of His Punishment: The Complete Collection
The Billionaire Next Door
The Millionaire and the Librarian
Riding with the Cop
Secret Desires of the Counselor
In Trouble with the Boss
Rough Ride with a Cowboy
Rough Day for the Teacher
A Forfeit for a Cowboy
Just what the Doctor Ordered
Wicked Romance of a Vampire

The Curve Collection: Big Girls and Bad Boys Series

The Curve Collection: The Complete Collection
The Curve Ball
The Beast Loves Curves
Curves by Design

Writing as Lane Parker

Dearest Stalker
Dearest Protector
A Christmas Dream
A Valentine's Dream
Lost: A Mountain Man Rescue Romance

A Dark Horse Novel w/ Cali MacKay

Bound
Hacked

Taken By A Trillionaire Series

Virgin for the Trillionaire by Ruth Cardello
Virgin for the Prince by J.S. Scott
Virgin to Conquer by Melody Anne
Prince Bryan: Taken By A Trillionaire

Other Titles

Well Played w/Ruth Cardello

.

Printed in Great Britain
by Amazon

61458771R00133